William Gotten was born and raised in Memphis, Tennessee. He graduated from Washington and Lee University with a B.A. degree and went on to get his J.D. degree from Cecil C. Humphreys School of Law in Memphis. He retired from the practice of Law in 2002 after over 30 years specializing in bankruptcy law. He continues to live in Memphis and enjoys writing. *Right of Survivorship* is his first book.

To my wife, Camille, who has doggedly demanded edits to establish her superior English education over mine, which she attributes to her public high school in Memphis.

I also wish to express appreciation to Carrie Beasley, who has devoted time and effort in implementing the demands of my wife's edits in the manuscript.

Thank you both.

William Gotten

William Gotten

RIGHT OF SURVIVORSHIP

AUSTIN MACAULEY PUBLISHERS™

LONDON • CAMBRIDGE • NEW YORK • SHARJAH

Ordering Information
Quantity sales: Special discounts are available on quantity purchases by corporations, associations, and others. For details, contact the publisher at the address below.

Publisher's Cataloging-in-Publication data
Gotten, William
Right of Survivorship

ISBN 9781638297840 (Paperback)
ISBN 9781638297857 (ePub e-book)

Library of Congress Control Number: 2022923458

www.austinmacauley.com/us

First Published 2023
Austin Macauley Publishers LLC
40 Wall Street, 33rd Floor, Suite 3302
New York, NY 10005
USA

mail-usa@austinmacauley.com
+1 (646) 5125767

The author wishes to express thanks to Attorneys P. Preston Wilson and Brian S. Faughnan for their advice and input as to certain legal issues referenced. The author is a retired lawyer who practiced bankruptcy law for 30 years.

Chapter 1

It was late when Sally Conners finished her grocery shopping at the Megamarket off Ridgeway Road, but she didn't mind doing her shopping at night since it was unlikely that she would see anyone she knew or anyone who would know her. She was glad about that as she really wanted to avoid having to answer prying questions if she did see anyone, which wasn't likely, since her neighbors didn't grocery shop at the Megamarket.

These were unpleasant times for her and her husband, Bob, what with all the financial problems that they were unhappily having to deal with. Financial problems brought arguments between them, which was something new in their relationship. She and Bob had been happily married and recently celebrated their 28th wedding anniversary.

Up until this year, they had been living pretty well on Bob's salary as a chemical engineer. They weren't rich by any means, but they had a nice house, lived in an upscale neighborhood and previously had few financial problems, even with their two children in private schools. The tuitions for the schools were expensive, but they sacrificed where they could to meet the costs and managed pretty well. Until this year and their subsequent need to have to file bankruptcy.

Sally really had not wanted Bob to file bankruptcy, but in her heart she knew they had no other choice. How long had it been now that Bob had been looking for a new job? Fourteen, no, fifteen months. There just weren't any jobs for a 53-year-old chemical engineer in Memphis, and his part time work at Walmart hadn't provided the income to do much of anything but pay the minimum on their credit card debt, which was huge. She was sure that Bob would eventually find another good paying job, but chemical companies still weren't hiring and his age was a "factor" in looking for work. The fact that he had had to file bankruptcy didn't help his résumé either. What was it the company had said? That they had to "cut back" after the merger so they were "downsizing" the staff. Twenty-two years of faithful work. Downsized.

Their lawyer said he had done what he could to keep the filing out of the papers, but all filings of bankruptcies were reported in the local business newspaper. It got out anyway. The neighbors all knew that something was seriously wrong at the Conners' house. Bob's company car was surrendered and Sally now drove a ten-year-old used Honda. At least they had been able to keep their house, though private school was no longer an option. The kids had taken that hard. With Sally working they were at least able to buy a used car for transportation after they had surrendered their cars to the bank.

Life presents challenges, she mused to herself, as she watched the checker put her groceries in the basket. Yeah, that's what their minister had said to them, that they would get through this; that they weren't the only ones who were being affected by the financial economic downturn. That didn't help much, but at least her family was intact and the kids were old enough to understand. Not happy by any means, but they understood the severe financial reversal and the effect it had had on their father. What had happened would be a lesson for them for sure not to take everything they had for granted.

Bob was so depressed. She knew he was doing all he could with a part-time job and looking every day for new employment. With her working, they were both worn out. No vacation, no time to themselves and their sex life had all but disintegrated along with their marriage. The kids hated public school and not seeing their friends in class.

All of these things were so weighing on her mind that she wasn't conscious of the car that drove out behind her from the parking lot, turning as she did, following her as she drove toward home down Ridgeway.

The road was dark and the bridge reconstruction that was under way was poorly lighted. There was a detour that required cars to drive over a temporary bridge that went over Nonconnah Creek, and the railings on the side wouldn't prevent a car from going over if the driver lost control. There were no lights in that section as she came to the bypass curve in the road. Bad enough in the daylight. Worse at night.

With her thoughts elsewhere, Sally never saw the big black Mercedes when it moved along beside hers on the curve of the roadway until it turned sharply into the driver's side of her car. Instantly, her thoughts went from her personal family concerns to panic. She had no control of the car! *Why was this happening?* She was heading off the road onto the embankment! Instinctively, she hit the brakes of the car, but now she was being pushed off the temporary road that led to the bypass bridge.

There was nothing to stop her! She screamed as her car went down the embankment into the swollen Nonconnah Creek. No one heard her screams. No one saw her car going down, down into the water. The Mercedes slowed, as the two men watched Sally's car sink into the icy river below. Slowly, they drove on as they saw the car sink under the river.

Chapter 2

Bob was watching television when the doorbell rang. He had become worried when Sally had not gotten home yet and the doorbell this late gave him concern. Sally had been so distraught lately and then somewhat distracted when she said that she needed to go to the grocery store. He knew she just needed to get away and cry to herself, away from him and the children, if only for a little while. It seemed like she did that a lot, now that their once comfortable and happy life had been shattered by the "downsizing" of his company. Downsizing! Such a palatable and "politically correct" term for ripping your life apart at his age.

He quietly seethed when he realized that no company wants a 53-year-old chemical engineer with a heart condition. Fifteen months now without a job that will support his family. He had been a vice-president with a good salary, benefits, company car and now he was minimum wage at Walmart. At least he got some medical health coverage, minimal as it was.

Fortunately, Sally had been able to get a job with Federal Express and for such time as it lasted, his 401K helped keep food on the table. He had to file bankruptcy! What else could he do? The credit card debt was enormous and got bigger every month with minimum payments. God, how did he let himself get so enmeshed in those credit cards! He had been such a fool to believe that nothing would change when the buyout talks began. Pushed out with stock options and an early retirement bonus. Yeah, that lasted long. Sounded good until he went out into the job market and faced reality.

The ringing of the doorbell snapped him back. *What time is it?* 10:30.

Who is calling at this hour? Maybe Sally forgot her key.

When he went to the door, he was disconcerted to see a man in a police uniform.

"Mr. Conners?" he asked.

"Yes, Officer, what can I do for you?" said Bob.

"I'm Sgt. Rainer with the Shelby County Sheriff's Office. Is your wife's name Sally Conners?" he asked.

"Yes, is there anything wrong? She's not here right now," said Bob.

"Sir, I'm afraid I have some bad news. There's been an accident on Ridgeway Road involving a woman with identification and a driver's license with that name. The car she was driving, well, she apparently lost control of the car and it went down an embankment. I'm sorry to have to tell you that the car went into Nonconnah Creek."

"But she's alright, isn't she? How badly was she hurt? Where is she? What hospital?" Bob said anxiously.

"No, Mr. Conners," replied Sgt. Rainer, "she's not all right. I'm sorry to have to tell you this, but evidently your wife was not able to get out of the car before it went into the river. You will need to come with us, please, sir, and we will take you to the crash site. The woman in the car, if she is

14

your wife, drowned and is dead. We need you to come identify the body."

Chapter 3

The black Mercedes sedan pulled into the motel parking lot and the two men got out and walked to the outside door. One of the men casually observed the damage to the right side of the car. He showed no concern or emotion for what they had done, nor did the other man. This is what they did. They killed people for money. Once inside, one of the men placed a call to the telephone number they had been given. The man didn't know who he was calling, but that was of no concern to him.

"Hello?" It was a man's voice. The telephone exchange was local, no area code required.

"The package has been delivered," said the larger man with no emotion.

"Any problems?" was the equally unconcerned reply.

"No," said the man.

"Good. The invoice for your services has been paid in the usual manner. Destroy this number," said the voice.

"Consider it done," was the reply.

The man picked up the slip of paper from the table and lighted it as he took a cigarette from his pocket and used the burning paper to light it. He drew deeply from his cigarette.

The other man said, "Do you want to do it now, or wait a couple of hours?"

"No," he said. "Let's do it now. You follow me."

"Okay," said the man as he stubbed out his cigarette.

As they left the motel room, one of the men went to a second car and pulled in behind the Mercedes as they drove onto Park Avenue. They would simply drive the scratched and dented car deep into downtown Memphis and leave it on the street in one of the projects. The man chuckled as he wondered how long it would stay there. He knew it wouldn't be long without being stolen. This was Memphis. Cars left alone on side streets were routinely stolen and if the police were able to make any connection with the Mercedes and the woman's, its occupants would be the prime suspects. No prints. No coffee cups. Nothing to connect the two men with the accident. Professional all the way. Or so they thought.

The man smiled thinking to himself that some young Black would probably wind up taking the fall if there was any tracing of the car to an investigation. *Serve him right for stealing the car*, he thought to himself. According to statistics, a lot of cars got stolen in Memphis. But he didn't think there would be any investigation. It was an accident, pure and simple. Woman lost control of her car on the bypass road. Not well lighted. No, there wouldn't be any homicide investigation. The woman drowned, end of story.

Chapter 4

The statistics of persons filing for personal bankruptcy are staggering.

In the U.S., over 1.3 million people a year attempt to wash away their financial difficulties by filing either a Chapter 7 or Chapter 13 bankruptcy petition. These are the two most usual choices under the Bankruptcy Code. These two chapters differ in many respects, but the main difference is the manner in which an individual's debts and assets are treated.

In a Chapter 13, the individual filing, called "the Debtor" proposes a plan for payment over an extended period of time, usually 36 months. The Debtor makes payments to a Chapter 13 Trustee on a regular basis, again according to the plan approved by the court and acquiesced to by creditors. The amount paid to creditors over the life of the plan is less than the full amount owed, but if the plan is completed, the remainder of whatever debt existed is "discharged," even though it may be a few cents on the dollar for creditors who had no security for payment of the debt or "unsecured" creditors. Usually, these are debts created by medical bills and charges the Debtor has made to credit cards or department stores.

"Secured" creditors have some type of security interest in property of the debtor, e.g., an automobile which is being bought "on time" through a purchasing contract. The security may also be an interest in "real property" meaning land, e.g., the debtor's house if he or she has one. Payment of the mortgage is provided for in the plan, provided the amount paid to the secured creditor is the full amount of the mortgage and the debtor has sufficient income to continue to pay the monthly amount due. Sometimes they can and sometimes they can't.

If the debtor cannot pay the monthly mortgage amount, then the secured creditor is entitled to file a motion to be able to foreclose on the property in order to be paid. If this motion is granted by the court, then the Debtor will have to make other living arrangements, and whatever equity in the property is lost upon foreclosure. Many times creditors work with the Debtor's attorney to find an amount the debtor can pay, as the secured mortgage holder often does not want to have to foreclose and possibly then have a property that it either cannot sell or may have difficulty in renting.

The success of the Chapter 13 plan depends on the Debtor's continued ability to pay the plan payment to the trustee. Often a Chapter 13 plan fails and the Debtor is then faced with converting the Chapter 13 bankruptcy into a Chapter 7 bankruptcy if he or she loses a job or simply cannot continue to have that much money taken from a paycheck and still provide for a family. If a Chapter 13 case is converted to a Chapter 7, then the assets of the Debtor, such as they may be, are turned over to a Chapter 7 Trustee, who is charged with the responsibility of marshaling those assets and liquidating them to pay creditors. Often there are no substantial assets to liquidate and the Trustee closes the case as a "no asset" case. The Debtor is then granted a discharge of all of the debts listed in the Chapter 7 petition and no longer owes the discharged debts.

Many times a Chapter 7 Debtor may have an interest in real property or in secured personal property, such as a car. In order to keep the car or the other secured property, the Debtor will have to either give up the property or reassume the debt in an amount that may be agreed to between the parties. If the Debtor does not or cannot reassume the debt, the property must be surrendered to the secured creditor, but if this happens, the remainder of the debt owed is discharged. This gives the Debtor what is called a "fresh start" free of past debt.

While this is the most usual event in a Chapter 7 bankruptcy, there are exceptions, especially where real property, such as a house, is involved and the Debtor and his or spouse own the property together, as one entity, under a deed describing a husband and wife as "tenants by the entirety," which is a legal term meaning that each spouse owns an interest in the real property based on their marriage to one another.

When the Debtor owns such a property with his or her spouse, and only one of the spouses files for bankruptcy, then the filing spouse's interest comes into the "bankruptcy estate" to be dealt with by the Chapter 7 Trustee. When the Trustee is faced with this situation, the interest of that spouse is essentially of no value, and the Trustee "disclaims" the interest that he may have as the Debtor's "successor in interest." This interest is called a "survivorship interest" and is only of value if there is a legal division between the spouses that affects the tenancy by the entirety.

While this interest held by the Chapter 7 Trustee is legally a salable interest, as mentioned, no one is going to buy it since it does not provide the buyer with any proprietary interest in the real property. The purchaser of the interest is not going to move in with the Debtor's spouse, even though, technically, a purchaser of the Trustee's interest does then own the Debtor's interest. If the purchaser of the Trustee's interest survives the non-filing spouse, then the buyer now owns the entire interest in the real property, the "fee simple," by operation of law and the whole of the property can be legally sold.

This "right of survivorship" that exists within the property that is owned by husband and wife as "tenants by the entirety" is Tennessee law, and may exist in the property laws of other states as well. This tenancy by the entirety is divisible only by a court having proper jurisdiction over the property as well as the husband and wife who own it by reason of their marriage. A bankruptcy court has such jurisdiction.

Chapter 5
Six Months Earlier

Bob and Sally felt that they had run out of options with their financial condition. Bob had talked in confidence with a lawyer friend of his and he suggested that Bob at least talk to a bankruptcy lawyer. He recommended Carter Manning.

"Oh, please," said Bob. "Tell me he's not one of those hustling lawyers I see on television all the time."

"No, he's not," replied his friend, Howard Stevens. "There are some good lawyers that handle bankruptcy cases, and I have known Carter for some time now. He does not advertise and I have referred many of my clients to him. It won't hurt to talk with him and see what he says. I'll give him a call and tell him to expect to hear from you."

"Okay, but Sally is going to freak out," said Bob.

Chapter 6

"Howard says he is a good lawyer and he specializes in bankruptcy cases, and, no, he is not an ambulance chaser or one of those lawyers you see on billboards or television," Bob said to Sally as they sat at their kitchen table. "I think we just need to get some advice. We are getting deeper in debt every month. All we are able to pay is just the minimum on the credit cards, and the interest is eating every spare dollar. I'm at my wits end and I can't find a decent paying job."

Sally couldn't have been more distressed with this conversation, but she recognized that Bob was right about their debt situation.

"So Howard knows this man?" asked Sally.

"Yes, and he says he has referred some of his clients to him. We can at least go and talk to him. There may be something we can do," said Bob.

"But bankruptcy, Bob, I don't know anyone who has filed bankruptcy. What if our friends or neighbors find out? I won't be able to hold my head up. And what about the house? Can we keep the house?" she said with tears beginning to form at the corner of her eyes.

"I don't know. That's why we need to get more information."

"But, Bob, we have put so much into this house. It's almost paid off, isn't it?"

"Yeah, almost," said Bob. "I think we still owe about $15,000. You know we could sell the house and pay off the debt we owe."

"I don't want to sell the house!" Sally said emphatically. "This is our home. The children would be heart broken, and so would I."

"I know," said Bob quietly. "I know. It was hard enough on their having to change schools, but we just couldn't afford that tuition."

"I really don't want to do this," Sally said.

"We can at least talk with the lawyer," said Bob.

Chapter 7

Carter Manning's office was in one of the high-rise office buildings in downtown Memphis. Howard had told them that he was a "sole practitioner," meaning that he practiced law by himself. Bob held the door for Sally as they went in. The office was nicely furnished and it gave the impression of a professional who evidently did well in his practice. Bob wasn't sure just what to expect from someone who made a living helping people who don't have any money. *Like he and Sally*, he thought to himself. They approached a nice woman attractively dressed, typing on a keyboard, who addressed them.

"Good afternoon. I'm Lisa, Mr. Manning's secretary," she said politely. "How may I help you?"

"We are the Conners," said Bob. "We are here for our appointment."

"Of course, Mr. Conners. Just one minute. Mr. Manning is expecting you."

Lisa buzzed Carter's office. "Mr. Manning, Mr. and Mrs. Conners are here for their two o'clock appointment," Lisa said.

"Thanks, Lisa," said Carter Manning. "Tell them I will be right out."

Carter Manning reached over for the calculator on his desk and picked up a yellow pad. He opened his desk drawer and pulled out a thick form stapled together for the interview. With his pad, calculator and form in hand, he walked down the office corridor to meet his new clients.

A lawyer acquaintance he knew, Howard Stevens, had called him and asked if he would talk to his friends, the Conners. Howard gave him a brief background of his association with Bob and Sally and said they were good friends of his that needed some financial advice. Howard told Carter that Bob had lost his job from being downsized from his company, which had recently gone through a merger with a larger chemical company.

"Hello, folks. I'm Carter Manning. How do you do?"

"Well," said Bob, "I guess we could be under better circumstances, Mr. Manning. You will have to tell us how we are doing and more importantly, what we should do. I'm Bob and this is my wife, Sally. She's not particularly happy being here."

"I understand that," Carter said. "I will try to answer your questions so we can decide what is the best thing to do under your particular circumstances. Won't you please follow me to my conference room and we will get started. I understand that you were referred to me by Howard Stevens and that he is a friend of yours. Howard is a fine lawyer and he has referred several of his clients to me."

"Yes," said Bob. "Howard is a neighbor and a good friend. We have known each other a long time. His wife is a friend of Sally's as well. I confided in him that we were having a difficult time financially. He knows that I was downsized from my company and have been looking for a job. Not much out there for a 53-year-old chemical engineer right now."

As a result of the interview, Carter learned that Bob was not the only senior staff employee that had been downsized, but on account of his age and medical history, he was not having any luck in finding another position as a chemical engineer. There were not that many petrochemical companies based in Memphis and though he had been provided with a generous severance pay when the merger went through, it was not the "golden parachute" that many senior employees received under similar circumstances, and the severance that Bob did get only lasted for so long. He lost his company car and many of the perks his company had provided went away as well, including his medical coverage.

Carter thought that Bob was typical for a man his age and education. He had had some cardiac problems and as a result of cardiac disease, he was required to have a stent and was on medication for his condition, but he was not what his cardiologist called a "severe risk" for a heart attack. Regardless, he was not a good risk when it came to seeking employment where medical coverage was concerned. This made him limited in the hiring pool, even though he was qualified in his field of expertise. His résumé, while impressive, limited him in many positions he applied for. He was either overqualified or "not what the hiring company was looking for."

Bob continued, "I was eased out of my job when my company was bought out after 22 years. I confess I'm a little bitter about that. I got a severance package and I thought it would see us through until I found other work in an executive capacity, but it hasn't, and now that money has been exhausted. I've been out of work for sixteen months now. There's not much of a labor market for a 53-year-old petrochemical engineer, at least, not in Memphis. I might find a job in Houston or Dallas, but we don't want to relocate. We like Memphis and this is Sally's hometown. We don't want to uproot our children either, but we had to take them out of private school, and they haven't taken that too well.

"I see," said Carter. "Are they in public schools now?"

"Yes," said Bob. "Our son, Bobby, is eight years old and is in Ridgeway Middle School. Our daughter, Elaine, is just starting the 10th grade and is at Ridgeway High School. Both schools are close to where we live. What can I say? They are public schools. They are not MUS and Hutchison, but we simply could not and cannot afford the tuitions. Both kids took the transfers badly. Their friends are still their friends, but they don't see them as much and, frankly, they are kind of embarrassed about our situation."

"Go on," said Carter. "This is good background information."

"Well, I have a part-time job at Walmart and I work about 28 hours a week. I can't work longer or I am told that they would have to consider me a full-time employee and provide medical coverage, which they can't or won't do because of my age and medical condition. The hospital allowed my cardiologist to perform the stent procedure, but the insurance did not pay all the expenses. I owe the hospital and my doctor, who has been very understanding of our situation, by the way, but I still owe him."

"A lot of my clients have medical bills," said Carter. "They are a primary reason for filing bankruptcy, but we will talk about that later."

"Sally has taken a job at FedEx in their billing department, which she likes and she is very competent now with the computer. She gets along well with others in the department, but the pay is not great. Together our income is just enough to get by with our monthly expenses, but we are not able to reduce our credit card debt and medical expenses. It's pay a little here and a little there, but that doesn't satisfy anyone. You can't imagine what it's like to go from making $150,000 dollars a year to $35,000."

"Believe me," said Carter. "I've been practicing my chosen profession for over ten years now and your situation is familiar. I have represented farmers who have had to give up property that has been in their family for three generations. It's not easy to have to explain that there is only so much that can be done. I'm not a miracle worker, but we can decide what is the best course of action in a particular case. I do know what you and your wife are going through."

"That's what I want to know," said Sally tearfully. "What do we have to give up. Will we lose our house?"

Carter replied, "Well, that depends on a lot of variables, but let me get some more information first. Like I said, one course of action may be better than another depending on your circumstances."

He felt pretty sure that a Chapter 7 or a "fresh start" was most likely what he would recommend, but a primary concern was their house.

From the interview, Carter had determined that the Conners did not owe any taxes, either federal, state or local, they were paying for one car on a monthly basis, they were meeting their mortgage payments thus far and they had an equity credit line that was manageable but not being reduced. They owed the Baptist Hospital for Bob's procedure, the doctor's bill for his cardiac care and over $40,000 in credit card debt, which, fortunately, was Bob's liability and not Sally's.

They had bought their house some twenty-two years ago for $76,500 in an area that was very desirable. They had a manageable mortgage, even though the amount paid into escrow had increased over the years as the property had become more valuable. Their residence was close to MUS and Hutchison, two private schools much in demand because of their reputations as excellent preparatory schools.

Carter explained that the house was security for the loan provided to the Conners by the mortgage company to buy their house. The bank that held their equity credit line was secured by the house as well. Both the mortgage company and the bank held Deeds of Trust signed at the time of the original purchase and the establishment of the equity credit line. He also explained that since they were still paying a monthly note on Sally's car, that it was likewise a secured debt.

"So the house is a secured debt," said Sally. "Does that mean that we will have to surrender the house if we file bankruptcy."

"Not necessarily," said Carter. "I will want to see the actual deed that you received when you bought the house, but in all likelihood, the house is owned by both you and Bob in the legal terminology of "tenants by the entirety.""

This means that both you and Bob own the house and the property it sits on. If only Bob files a Chapter 7 bankruptcy, technically, and legally, only his interest comes into the "bankruptcy estate."

When a husband and wife own real property, by which I mean land, by the entireties, it is a type of joint ownership specific to the marital relationship. Should Bob predecease you, Mrs. Conners, that property becomes solely owned by you, in what is legally called "fee simple." Same with Bob should you predecease him."

"Now here is where it gets a little complicated," said Carter. "If only one of the spouses files a Chapter 7 bankruptcy, only that spouse's interest becomes an asset that has to be included in the petition. Legally, that asset passes to the Chapter 7 Trustee, but he is not going to move into the house with you, and generally, he considers the property interest to be of no value, though it is a salable asset. If the bankruptcy petition has no other assets which can be liquidated to pay creditors, then the Trustee will generally consider the case to be a "no asset" case and he can administer the case in short order. The Debtor, in this case the filing spouse, receives a discharge of all of the debts he or she has listed in the petition, assuming that there is no reason for a creditor to object to the discharge of that creditor's debt for some reason, such as fraud in the making of the debt."

"But we don't owe very much on our house," said Bob, "in fact I think it is less than $15,000 on the mortgage and $10,000 on the equity credit line, which you say is secured by the house, is that right?"

"Yes," said Carter, "the bank's equity credit line is secured by the house. If you don't pay the promissory note you both signed when that loan was taken out, the bank has legal options it can take to satisfy that obligation. The bank holds a second lien on the house, which is subject to the mortgage company's first lien. Legally, the bank could foreclose on the house, pay the first lien holder, your mortgage company, and sell the house for its value."

"So what do we do about that debt? We don't want to lose our house," said Sally. "We've lived in that house for twenty-two years. It's our home."

"I understand completely," said Carter, "but let me finish. You don't both need to file. Bob can 'reaffirm' that debt, that is to say, he agrees to continue to pay the balance of the mortgage and the equity credit line by making a new promise to pay the debt. If Bob does this, then in all likelihood, you will be able to keep your house."

"What do you mean 'in all likelihood'?" said Bob. "Can we not demand to be allowed to reaffirm the debt?"

"Sadly, no, you can't," said Carter. "Reaffirmation is entirely up to the creditor, but in almost all cases, the bank and the mortgage company will allow a reaffirmation of their debt. Why? Because they really don't want to have to deal with disposing of the property by going through a foreclosure. However, you have had your house for a long time and you have built a lot of equity, which is why you probably had no trouble at all taking out an equity credit line. The bank is over secured for the amount of its loan. As the owners of the property, you and your husband would be entitled to a homeowners' exemption allowed by the State of Tennessee, which is $7,500. That's not very much."

"So under that premise," said Bob, "if I understand you, we would only get $7,500 from whatever the Trustee realizes net from the sale?" We only owe about $25,000 in secured debt on the house, and I would say that a fair market value of our house would be in excess of $300,000. That's not the value for tax appraisal, it's a lot less, but not a whole lot less, and the house down the street just sold for $315,000. That means that we have a lot of equity."

"Indeed you do," replied Carter, but, again, if you own the house together as husband and wife as tenants by the entirety, only your interest, Bob, if you file, comes into the bankruptcy estate, and as we have discussed, the Chapter 7 Trustee considers this survivorship interest to be of no or certainly limited value. While salable, who's going to buy an interest in property that they can't occupy, can't sell, can't evict the other spouse, and will, in all likelihood, lose their investment if the spouse who filed dies first. Their investment then goes up in smoke since the non-filing spouse legally owns the property in his or her name. It's a gamble that may or may not pay off in however many years."

"I have to confess," said Bob, "that the idea of losing our house and only getting $7,500 does not appeal to me. Will Sally be required to file?"

"No," said Carter, "she cannot be required to file and as long as she has no liability on the unsecured debt, she is free from any lawsuit to collect. We need to make sure of that."

"So as long as we continue to pay the mortgage and the equity credit line in a satisfactory manner, assuming that we can reaffirm those obligations, we keep the house and we won't owe any of the unsecured debt, is that right?"

"Yes, and the Chapter 7 petition will discharge you from that debt, but you do want to get a confirmation from the bank and the mortgage company that they will allow the debt to be reaffirmed. And, of course, I need to see your Warranty Deed to make sure that you and Sally own the house as tenants by the entirety."

"The concept of tenants by the entirety for a husband and wife is based on the spouses being joined in holy matrimony, that is, the church, says that they become one entity, and the law has adopted this. This, in turn, creates the "right of survivorship" at death and the legal concept that a wife cannot dispose of her interest in the property and the husband cannot dispose of his interest, or his wife's interest without her written consent and vice versa," Carter explained.

"But a court can, is that right?"

"Yes," said Carter.

"And whoever survives the other by death, gets the property in their own name?" asked Bob.

"Yes, whoever survives gets the property by operation of law and nothing further is required. No deed, no Last Will or other document is required. Indeed, it would wreak havoc on the states' property laws where this legal fiction exists," said Carter, "and many states have this in their property laws."

"Well, you have given us a lot to think about," said Bob.

"We will need to confirm the things we talked about, however, before proceeding," said Carter. "Can you bring me your Warranty Deed on the house?"

"Yes," said Bob, it's in our safe deposit box at the bank. I guess I will have an opportunity to speak with the branch manager at the same time."

"Good," said Carter. "Well, until next time. Any other questions?"

"No, not from me," said Bob. "Sally?"

"No," she said rather tearfully.

Chapter 8

The office of Worthmore Financial is in a nondescript building on White Station Road in Memphis. The building holds the offices of several medical and dental practices as well as personal offices of various entities that few people have ever heard of. It is ideal for individuals who want an office to go to from time to time to get away from home and have an office address for whatever business someone might want to conduct. The ground floor has a bank of mail boxes for the postman to put mail in so he doesn't have to knock on doors for delivery of mail to the occupants who often are not there.

Worthmore, therefore, by design, keeps a low profile, doesn't advertise any financial services, doesn't have regular customers with whom it provides routine banking services, offers no checking accounts or loans, despite its name as a financial business of some kind. It has no telephone listing in the Memphis directory and information on Google is sparse, lists no officers or employees or services offered.

One would simply not know it exists, which is the way the man who rented the office wanted it. Worthmore is not a corporation and therefore has no filing with the State of

Tennessee. It has no Federal Employer Identification number (E.I.), has no employees. It reports no income and pays no taxes. It is, in fact, a ghost, but that does not matter to the landlord who gets his rent promptly every month. What is done or not done in that office is of no concern to him. He doesn't get any complaints and he likes it that way. A telephone number given to him is answered by an answering machine with the simple message, "leave a number." A public finance company it is not.

Chapter 9

After the Bankruptcy

"So how long do we wait," said the heavy-set man into the telephone.

"That depends, came the reply. "It's better to wait five or six months. Less chance of any connection. It needs to look like an accident and I think I have a plan for that. You will need another man."

"Okay," the other said. "I'll bring Rocco when it's time. Call me."

Chapter 10

Present Day

Lt. Harvey Martin of the Detective Division of the Memphis Police Department scratched his chin as he looked over the report of the accident on Ridgeway Road. Since it involved a death, but not clearly a homicide, he was encouraged to not waste valuable Department time by his Captain. However, he was uncomfortable doing that and his instincts as a detective told him that it just didn't make sense to him how the car went over the embankment the way the report indicated. True, the road was under construction for the new bridge and the detour wasn't well lighted. And there wasn't any barricade to prevent a car from going over the embankment, but what made the woman lose control?

The autopsy and medical report from the coroner didn't indicate any residue of alcohol or drugs in her body, and the accident happened at a time when there most likely were very few cars on the road. From a review of the woman's driving record, there was no indication of reckless driving, not even a speeding ticket in the last five years, yet she had apparently lost control of the car. She had not had a heart attack or any other medical event according to the autopsy that would have caused her to black out or lose consciousness. Besides, she had drowned, so she was alive and conscious when the car went into the river. Weather was not a factor. Streets were clear.

The accident might have been just that. An accident as a result of unknown causes. Happens all the time, people lose concentration on what they're doing while driving. But he was a detective for a reason, and a good one. He didn't like to just put the death of a healthy woman aside, especially a wife and a mother of two children with no immediate contributing factor. He dialed the Property Division's Impound Lot number.

"Hey, this is Lt. Martin, Detective Squad. Who's this?" he said.

"Hi. L.T., this is Jensen. What can I do for you?"

"I'm looking at an accident report from last night involving a single car that was pulled from Nonconnah Creek, said Martin. "It's a 2009 Honda Civic, green in color, license number BDH-812. Is it somewhere on the lot?"

"Yeah, L.T., it's here," replied Jensen. "Getting dried out before we release it. Registered to a Robert Conners. I understand that's the name of the husband of the woman who was in the car at the time, so I'm told. Drowned in the accident, so I was told. He's coming to claim it. Damn sad."

"Does it have any damage?" asked Martin. "According to the report it just went over the embankment and down into the creek."

"Yeah, L.T.," said Jensen, "it does have a scrape and dent on the driver's side. Looks new to me. I'm sure the owner is going to say we did it pulling it out of the river, but we didn't. A-1 Salvage got the call and they reported the damage to us. Guess they don't want to be accused of doing it either."

"Okay," said Martin. "Look, can you take some pictures of the damage, and don't release it until I can come take a look at it."

"Got that, L.T. Will do. When you coming?" said Jensen.

"Now. By the way, did you check the brakes or steering or anything mechanical?" Martin asked.

"Nah, L.T.," replied Jensen. "Do you know how many cars come in here in a day? We ain't got time to see what kind of mechanical condition they're in, and don't really care. We inventory them in and get a receipt for the tow. Most of them get claimed within twenty-four hours unless they're junk. People want their rides back, L.T., you know what I mean?

"I did hear the A-1 driver say that he put his foot on the brakes after they pulled it. Nothing wrong with the brakes or the steering as far as we know, but it hasn't had a full mechanical check. We can't do that with every car we impound," replied Jensen.

"Okay," said Martin, "but I want to rule out anything mechanical. Something doesn't seem right. I'll be there in twenty."

Chapter 11

"Dad, what happened? Mom was always a good driver," said Bobby. His eyes were red from crying so much.

His father said, "I don't know, Bobby. She evidently lost control of the car. You know that place over on Ridgeway, near Mt. Moriah. They're putting in a new bridge and there is a detour over to a temporary bridge over the river. I just don't know." Bob was just as sad as his son.

"What's going to be done with the car? Do we get it back?" asked Bobby.

"Oh, sure," said Bob. "In fact, I got a call about it. It's in the police impound lot drying out. I'll have to go get it and have it cleaned up. The man said it was full of muddy water."

"I'm not sure I want it back," said Bobby, his eyes starting to moisten again. "Not ever."

"I know Bobby," his father replied, "but we need the car."

"Dad, could anything have gone wrong with the car?" asked Bobby. "Maybe the brakes or something. It's not like it was a new car."

"I think the car was in good mechanical condition," Bob said. "I've thought about that too, but I looked up the repair records and it was in the shop a couple of months ago for a 75,000-mile check. They did a pretty thorough check on all of the car, brakes, transmission, tires and all the other things that are done on that mileage, but when we get it back, I will take it to the dealership just to make sure that the brakes and the steering didn't have anything to do with Mom losing control."

"When do we get it back?" asked Bobby.

"I'll call about it when we get back from the funeral home," said Bob, "but now it's time to go. Is your sister ready?"

"Yeah, I think so," said Bobby. "She's still crying though."

"We will get through this, son, but right now we just have to do what we have to do," Bob said sadly.

Bob tried to keep his composure and be strong for his children, but he was really worried. Funerals cost a lot of money, and that was something they were pretty short of right now. He knew that there was a small life insurance policy on Sally's life that he hoped would cover the funeral expenses.

He thought about the loss of Sally's income from FedEx and his bankruptcy, now six months ago. He still had not been able to find a replacement job as a chemical engineer in Memphis, but he at least was now working full time at Walmart and had gotten a second job at an accounting firm that allowed him to work at home. He wondered if he could ask for Sally's job at FedEx since they would need a replacement. He was pretty sure that he could do what she did. He also thought that maybe he could get a job in Houston or Dallas, sell the house and just move.

"Dad?"

"Yes, Bobby."

"Do we need to talk to a lawyer, maybe Mr. Manning? asked Bobby. "I mean isn't the city responsible for the condition of the road if that caused her to lose control and go over the embankment?"

"I don't know, Bobby," his father answered. "We really don't know what happened, but I suppose it wouldn't hurt to talk to Mr. Manning. Now, go get your sister. The cab will be here any minute."

Chapter 12

"You read about the car going over the embankment on Ridgeway, right," asked Asst. City Attorney Evans Shappley to his boss.

"Yeah," said City Attorney, Martin Brownley. "What does it look like to you?"

"It's hard to say," Shappley said. "I'm familiar with the area since I don't live too far from there. I thought I would take another look at it again on my way home tonight. I know it was a bad place on account of the detour and the area wasn't well lighted. I hate to say it was an accident waiting to happen, but someone has some exposure and it is a city street."

"But it isn't a city project, I mean it was farmed out to a construction company, wasn't it?" asked Brownley.

"Yeah, but still," said Shappley, "we are going to get our tail in a ringer. The woman died. Drowned. A wife and a mother coming home from the grocery store at 10 o'clock according to the story."

"If they sue, then we will see," said Brownley. "Didn't the article in the paper show a picture of the bridge area? Doesn't look good because it was so dark and the picture just emphasized that. Why didn't MLG&W have better lighting in that area?"

"Don't know," said Shappley. "Have to ask them. I'm sure they will say it's not their project and it was the construction company's responsibility. Going to be a lot of finger pointing, I imagine."

"That's for sure," said Brownley. "Someone dropped the ball, although there were plenty of flashing barricade lights."

"Yeah, that will be a great defense when you've got a forty-three-year-old mother of two who goes over an embankment and drowns. No chance that's in Germantown, is it," Shappley said with a grin.

"No, unfortunately not. It's close to the city boundary out there, I mean the city limits line meanders, but it's our jurisdiction," replied the City Attorney.

"Well, *The Commercial Appeal* is all over this and I expect we will be hearing from some attorney pretty soon. You better leave early and go see it in the daytime, and then get some pictures when it gets dark. What, it gets dark about 5:30 now?" asked Brownley.

"Oh, yeah. It's plenty dark then," replied Shappley.

"And find out what you can about how the accident happened. If we can show that it was caused by something other than poor lighting conditions, we might be able to dodge the bullet," said Brownley.

Chapter 13

A Day Earlier

"So, what happens now," said the other man who was in the Mercedes.

"That's really not any of our concern, Rocco," was the reply from the heavy-set man as he stubbed out his cigarette. "We've been paid and we're out of it. No problems. Don't ask too many questions. We're leaving. Are you packed up?"

"Okay," said the other. "I'm ready. Too bad we can't take the Mercedes. That was a nice car."

Chapter 14

Lt. Martin examined the driver's side of the Honda Civic. The dent in the door and scraping was immediately evident to anyone's observation. The paint scrape was black on a green car and it clearly looked fresh even after being in the water.

"So, what does that look like to you, Jensen?" said Martin.

"Well, L.T.," Jensen said, "I would say that the car had been kinda side-swiped by a black car, but, hey, you're the detective."

"You don't have to be a detective to figure that one out," replied Martin, grinning at Jensen's tongue-in-cheek comment. "Now, where's the other car that hit it?"

"You're not going to believe this Lt., but a black Mercedes with damage to the right front fender was pulled off Georgia Avenue and came into the lot last night. It was reported stolen two days ago and it was just waiting to be stolen again where it was found. Patrol found it pretty quickly on Georgia Avenue. Now who is going to leave a Mercedes in that area? Wasn't locked. Valid license and registration, reported stolen by the owner two days ago. Kids joy riding, you think?" asked Jensen.

"Is it still here?" asked Martin.

"As a matter of fact, it is, according to the log. Owner hasn't come to pick it up. Says here it belongs to a Wesley Thompson. Lives in East Memphis," said Jensen. "He's been called and advised we have found his car."

"Where is it? I want to see it," said Martin.

"Sure, L.T., you think it might have been the other car in this accident," replied Jensen.

"If it is, then this was no accident. It was a hit and run."

Jensen took Martin to the Mercedes on the lot. On the passenger side, it was scraped and the front fender dented. The green paint showed up prominently against the black paint on the front fender of the Mercedes.

"Holy shit. Will you look at that?" said Jensen. This may be the car that hit the Honda."

"Yeah, how about that. Get the camera and take some more pictures. I'm calling in to get a search warrant, and give me the owner's telephone number. He may have some explaining to do," said Martin.

"You got it, L.T.," said Jensen.

"And hang on to this car. I want prints," said Martin.

Chapter 15

Martin didn't have much to go on to get a search warrant for the Mercedes, but the circumstances of what he thought was not an accident and a sympathetic judge got what he wanted. He went back to the car on the impound lot and with the help of latent prints dusted the car inside and out. Danny with the lab said there were no prints and the car had been wiped clean, but with one exception.

There were two cigarette butts in the ashtray and they both had a smudge of a print when dusted. Neither one of the butts was enough to make a positive ID, but it was evidence none the less and together, the latent print lab tech thought they might be able to get part of a print from each butt and they would work on it. The brand was Marlboro, a very common brand, but the ashtray otherwise looked unused.

They had better luck with the paint from the Mercedes on the Honda. It was a match, which told Martin with some certainty that these two cars had collided, presumably where Sally Conners lost control of her car. Had someone deliberately hit the Civic causing it to go over the embankment? If so, this made it a homicide in Martin's book, but could he prove it and who was driving the car?

If, as Jensen thought, a young teenager had decided to steal the car and go joy riding, why would the car be left on the side of the road on Georgia Avenue in the hood and wiped clean? Would a teenager or teenagers do that? He didn't think so. Also, patrol said the car was unlocked when they had it towed in. Could whoever have stolen the car also been the one driving it when the other car went over the embankment?

Martin's gut and experience told him that it was highly unlikely that a joy-riding teen would have taken the time to wipe the car clean if he was driving the car when it hit the Honda and even if he did, he would have been so scared that in his haste to remove any evidence, he was bound to have missed some of his prints. No, this car was wiped completely. A purposeful cleaning. And, it had not been hot-wired.

Martin knew that it wasn't hard to steal a Mercedes, or any car, for that matter, but there was no sign that the ignition had been jimmied like an amateur thief might do. Things just didn't add up to him thus far.

Martin had asked Jensen to call him when Wesley Thompson showed up to claim his car, which he did, and that gave him a quick chance to get over to the lot and ask the owner some questions.

After introductions, Martin asked, "Mr. Thompson, do you smoke?"

"Well, that's a strange question, Detective, but no, I don't smoke," he replied.

"Do you know why we found two cigarette butts in the ashtray of your car? Has there been anyone in your family that might have used the car recently that smokes?" asked Martin.

"No, and the car has been in my possession up until the time that it was stolen. More than likely, whoever stole the car smoked," said Thompson.

"You reported the car stolen two days ago. Where was it when it was stolen?" asked Martin.

"In my driveway at my residence. I knew immediately when it was gone and called the police," replied Thompson. "I gave all this information to the officers that responded to my call."

"Routine questions, sir. Does anyone else in your family or otherwise have keys to the car?" Martin asked.

"No. I have a son, but he is away at college, and he would certainly not have taken the car without my knowledge, and he is 500 miles away," replied Thompson indignantly. "Perhaps whoever stole the car smoked, have you thought of that."

"Yes, sir, we have. Have you examined the damage to the car?" Martin asked.

"Yes, I have, and it was not damaged before it was stolen, I can assure you of that. Is that what this is about? Was the car in an accident after it was stolen?" asked Thompson.

"It is certainly possible," said Martin. "We need to remove the front panel and passenger side door of the car. Would that be all right with you? We believe your car was involved in a homicide and we are investigating whether it was an accident."

Chapter 16

The Bankruptcy Court Clerk's office for the Western District of Tennessee, Western Division in Memphis, is the model of efficiency, something that the Clerk and the Bankruptcy Judges were proud of. Lawyers can file their bankruptcy petitions in person at the intake counter or on line. The cases are promptly assigned a number and a Bankruptcy Judge, and the required copies set aside for those entities who receive copies. Two copies went to the United States Trustee, who then assigns an attorney from the pool of Asst. U. S. Trustees that handle the cases filed. The original petition stays in the court file, the clerk requires an additional copy for "administration and training" and the remaining copies are for the attorney filing for the Debtor.

All in all, there are a lot of copies of the petitions filed, each one containing much personal information. The names of the person or persons, if filing jointly, who filed and their property. This information is actually public information and anyone who wants to come into the Clerk's office and look at any particular petition can do so, if they have the number of the case or the Debtor's name.

The Debtor's Social Security Number, address, assets, value of assets, type of property, whether married or not, the status of the marriage, the Debtor's place of employment, income and much more. A cornucopia of information is in the petition if a person looking for certain information was doing so for purposes other than that related to an action by or for a creditor.

Or someone in possession of, or access to, a petition could simply provide this information to a third party for any number of reasons.

People who file bankruptcy generally are not proud of having to do so and do not want this known. It is easy to know, however, who has filed and what assets and debts are owed as the local business newspaper prints the names, case numbers and amount shown for assets and liabilities stated in the petitions.

Worthmore Financial likes to have this information.

Chapter 17

"L.T., this is Jensen, over at the impound lot. You wanted me to hold the Honda Civic that was involved in the crash you are investigating, right?"

"Yeah, definitely, and I haven't had a chance to talk to the owner, yet. Conners, isn't it?" asked Martin.

"That's right, a Robert Conners, and the reason I'm calling is because he is here and wants to pick up the car. I told him you had a hold on it. You want to talk to him?" asked Jensen.

"Yes," said Martin, "put him on the line."

"Hello. This is Bob Conners. Who is this?"

"This is Detective Harvey Martin with the East Precinct of the Memphis Police Department, Mr. Conners. I am very sorry for the loss of your wife, sir, and I need to just ask a few questions, if you don't mind."

"You are a detective?" asked Bob.

"Yes, sir, and I am investigating the crash that resulted in the death of your wife."

"What do you want to know, Detective?" asked Bob warily.

"To begin with," said Martin, "was there any damage to your car before this event, especially on the driver's side of the car?"

"No, detective," said Bob. "There was no damage at all to the car. I've seen it now and none of this damage was there. Why do you ask? Do you think that another car may have caused this damage? From what I have been told, the car went over the embankment because, perhaps, my wife lost control somehow. I intend to take it to the dealership where we bought it and have the steering and the brakes checked out. It wasn't a new car, but it was in good condition and it had been serviced not too long ago. I take care of my cars or rather, my cars, when I had two. This is the only one I have right now and I need to get it back."

"I understand, sir, and it is good that you intend to check out the mechanical condition of the car, but I have already had one of our mechanics do a cursory check at my request, and he said that there was, or is, nothing wrong with either the brakes or the steering. Frankly, sir, we are not sure why the car your wife was driving went off the road," said Martin.

"I don't know either, detective. The coroner said that she didn't have a heart attack and she didn't have any alcohol in her system," related Bob.

"Sally would have a glass of wine from time to time on our patio, but she was not a drinker and she certainly didn't use any drugs. She doesn't, or rather didn't, even take any medicines, I mean prescription drugs. I would know."

"Yes, sir, I know what the report said. That's one of the things that bothers me about this event," said Martin. "We don't know what happened and I'm not ready to call it an accident."

"What are you saying, Detective? Do you think she was run off the road? Even if another car hit hers, wouldn't that be an accident," queried Bob, with some concern in his voice.

"We are simply looking into the cause of the car going over the embankment, sir," said Martin. "Don't read anything into the investigation, but I do want to make a request, if you don't mind."

"What is that?" replied Bob.

"We would like to preserve the fender and door of the car. They have some black paint on these pieces and we need to do a paint match with another car that we suspect might have been involved," said Martin.

"Does that mean you are going to remove the door and the front panel of the car? I just said I need my car back. I can't drive it around without a driver's side door," said Bob somewhat angrily.

"Well, we are just asking if we may keep the car for another day and compare the dent and scrape. That way we will be able to prove one way or the other that this other car was or was not involved in the crash," replied Martin.

"You can do this in a day?" asked Bob.

"Yes, sir, if we have your permission," replied Martin. "The owner of the other car has already given his permission. We want to match the markings up and, as I said, test the paint samples of each car."

"Wait," said Bob. "You have the other car? Was the owner driving the car?"

"Right now we don't know who was driving the car," replied Martin. "The owner says it was stolen, and it was found abandoned."

"Well, you've asked him if he was driving the car, didn't you?" queried Bob.

"Yes, sir, and he has denied driving the car at the time of the event," replied Martin.

"You keep saying 'event,' Detective," said Bob. "Why can't you say accident? Two cars hit one another. Isn't that an 'accident?'"

"Yes, sir, it can certainly be described that way," said Martin.

"Well, I have a right to know," said Bob angrily. "Do you think it was an accident, or more to the point, why do you think it wasn't an accident?"

"I can't make any definitive call on that, sir. The car was reported stolen, it was in a crash with another car, we believe your wife's car, then left abandoned, and wiped clean of fingerprints. That's unusual for a car that was stolen for joy riding or for whatever purpose it was stolen. A car like this one would be stripped to its skeleton in a few hours where it was abandoned. Fortunately, a routine patrol found it and had a report that it had been reported stolen. This was the same night of your wife's death and within an hour of whatever caused her to lose control of the car," replied Martin.

Chapter 18

"Mr. Manning," said Lisa as Carter came into the office. She had a questioning tone to her voice.

"Yes, Lisa, good morning. Something up?" he said.

"Well, yes, I guess and maybe not, but I thought if you haven't seen the paper, you might have missed this story."

"What story?" replied Manning.

"Well, you remember our clients from about six months ago, the Conners? You filed a Chapter 7 no asset bankruptcy petition for him. He had lost his job or something. A real nice middle-aged couple?"

"Yes, Lisa, I remember them," said Carter.

"Well, in the paper this morning is a story about a car going over the embankment on Ridgeway and into Nonconnah Creek," said Lisa.

"Okay," said Carter patiently, waiting for Lisa to get to the point.

"Well, Mrs. Conners was in that car," said Lisa.

"What? Really? That's terrible. Is she okay?" asked Carter.

"No," Lisa said. "She's dead. Drowned in the creek. The paper says she couldn't or didn't get out of the car. I thought you would want to know."

"Indeed. Thank you," replied Carter.

Chapter 19

Tommy Barton, the MPD lab technician, called Lt. Martin. "L.T., this is Tommy down at the lab. I have checked the paint samples that you brought in. They match. I thought you would want to know as soon as I was able to confirm the test. The paint from the Mercedes is a particular type of high quality only used on Mercedes automobiles, so that wasn't very difficult. I can say without a doubt that the paint taken from the Honda Civic door and front panel came from the Mercedes."

"Okay, Tommy," replied Martin. "Thanks. Write it up for me, will you?"

"Sure. You going to hold on to the cars?" asked Barton.

"With confirmation from the body repair shop that the dent in the Honda was caused by the Mercedes hitting it and your paint confirmation match, I think we can probably return the cars to the owners," replied Martin. "Now all we have to do is find who was driving the Mercedes when it hit the Honda, and of course, what happened and perhaps why."

Chapter 20

Carter Manning picked up his telephone and punched in the number for the U.S. Trustee's Office.

"United States Trustee's Office, may I help you."

"Cindy, this is Carter Manning. Is Robbie there by any chance?" he asked.

"I believe he is, Mr. Manning. Hold on and I will buzz him for you," Cindy replied.

"Robert Easton."

"Hey, Robbie. This is Carter. Have you got a second?"

"Sure, Carter, my man. What's up?" replied Easton.

"You handled a Chapter 7 bankruptcy case about six months ago for one of my clients, a Robert Conners. It was a no asset case, fairly routine. Do you remember it?" Carter asked.

"Yeah, I do, but it wasn't a no asset case. Very unusual as I recall, which is why I remember the name."

"It wasn't?" asked Carter surprised at the comment.

"Well, it was and it wasn't, I suppose," replied Easton. "The debtor had a pretty large equity interest in his home place as I recall. About $250,000, but it was owned by him and his wife as tenants by the entirety, so as in so many other similar cases, I was going to sign off and disclaim the Trustee's interest.

"And you didn't?" Carter asked. "I never heard anything about it one way or the other." He was a little miffed. "Why not?"

"Now don't get all riled up," said Easton. "I got a call from a finance firm I never heard of, Worthmore Financial, and this representative asked if the Trustee's interest was for sale."

"So you're talking about the right of survivorship interest that passes to the Trustee?" asked Carter.

"Yeah, in all my years as a Chapter 7 Trustee, I never had anyone ask about buying the Trustee's position in a tenancy by the entirety interest," said Easton. "I asked this guy did he know that the interest of the Trustee gave him essentially nothing, no right of occupancy, that the interest would most likely not be resalable to a third party in order to get his money back and that it was also likely that he or his company would lose whatever investment he was willing to make to buy the survivorship interest, and he said, yes, he knew all that, but that he thought someday it might pay off."

"So, how did you handle it?" said Manning.

"Well, first I asked him how much he expected to pay for it and was he a gambler. I really didn't think much of the idea, especially if, as he said, he was with a "financial" institution, but he said he wasn't a bank," replied Easton.

"Sounds squirrely to me," said Manning.

"Yeah, I thought so too, but he said he would pay $1,000 for it and he wanted a Quit Claim Deed that he could file to evidence his, or rather, Worthmore's interest, in the property. Well, anyway, I asked around the office and no one else had ever sold a Chapter 7 Trustee's interest. Hayes said he had an inquiry one time, but when he told the person who said he was interested that he got essentially nothing, he cooled on the idea," said Easton.

"So, did you do it?" asked Manning.

"Yeah, I did. I got a cashier's check for $1,000 and a Quit Claim Deed, which I signed and mailed back. The envelope that was included with the check and deed just had a Post Office box address, which I thought was strange for a financial company, I mean, no printed return address, but the check was good. I paid the administrative expenses on the case, got a small fee approved by the Court and made a distribution to the creditors with the remainder. Wasn't much. Really more trouble than it was worth, but, ha ha, it was worth more to Worthmore, I guess, pun intended. The unsecured creditors got a pro-rata portion. The Debtor had already reaffirmed the secured debt to the mortgage company and to the bank that had an equity credit line on the property," said Easton.

"Why wasn't I advised of this?" asked Manning angrily.

"Well," replied Easton, "I didn't think anything about it. I guess I could have called you and maybe I should have. I was busy and it didn't matter since the interest is only a possibility of an *in futuro* claim. I got the money, signed the deed, paid the creditors and closed the case. The Debtor got his discharge. Why are you asking about it?"

"Because it may not be a future interest. In fact, it is a very real and current interest," replied Manning.

"What? What are you saying?" said a concerned Easton.

"Mrs. Conners is dead," replied Manning, "and the interest you sold to Worthmore Financial, the survivorship interest, is now a real and present interest. If the transfer by your Quit Claim Deed holds up, Worthmore now has an ownership interest in my client's house. If Worthmore pays off the first mortgage and the balance of the equity credit line, around $25,000 total as I remember, it gets a full ownership interest in a house worth over $300,000. It could net about $275,000 or more for its $1,000 "investment.""

"You got to be shitting me!" exclaimed Easton.

"No, no, I'm not. And I'm the one who is going to have to tell my client, who just lost his wife, that he is probably going to have to move out of his home," Manning said sadly. "Not a happy prospect."

"Jesus!" said Easton.

Chapter 21

Carter Manning was angry that Robbie Easton had not let him know of the sale of Bob Conner's survivorship interest, not that he could have done much about it since it was the Chapter 7 Trustee's call, but this was the first time he had ever heard of an interest being sold, and who the hell was Worthmore Financial? He Googled the name and was really surprised when nothing came up. If Google didn't have anything, not even an address or telephone contact, that was really strange. He picked up the phone and called an acquaintance at *The Commercial Appeal*, Tom Watson.

"Watson," was the answer he got when he called the number.

"Tom, this is Carter Manning. I don't know if you remember me, but you did an article on bankruptcy a while back and I was a source you interviewed. I'm the bankruptcy attorney."

"Oh, sure. I remember you," Watson said. "You gave me some really good information for that article. What's on your mind?"

"Well, this is something really unusual, and since you are an investigative reporter of sorts, I thought I would see what you can come up with. It involves a financial institution that bought my client's survivorship interest in his house following his filing a bankruptcy," said Carter.

"Okay, I'm game. What's a survivorship interest?" he replied.

Carter took a couple of minutes to explain the real property concept of a tenancy by the entirety interest of a husband and wife, and the interest of a spouse who files bankruptcy owning real property. He explained how unusual it was that anyone would want to put money into buying an interest that was nothing more than a gamble.

"Well, that is interesting. How many times did you say this has happened?" asked Watson.

Carter replied, "That's just it, never in my experience, and only this once in this bankruptcy district to anyone's knowledge. I checked, and here's something else that is interesting, I can't find any information on this company that bought it."

"What did you say the name was, something financial?" asked Watson.

"Yeah," said Carter, 'Worthmore Financial' and according to the Chapter 7 Trustee, it has a P.O. Box for an address. What financial institution doesn't have a street address, a telephone number or a website?"

"Okay," said Watson, "they or it doesn't act like a bank or financial institution. So what? It could just be an individual that has that name for his own investment portfolio. That wouldn't be that unusual, and if it is an individual, that would explain having a P.O. Box for an address. He's not a bank and doesn't make loans, or maybe he does. Maybe that's what the business is, a private financial entity with a low profile."

"That could be," said Carter, "but Worthmore bought this survivorship interest for $1,000 with a cashier's check and now stands to rake in a lagniappe of about $275,000. I'm wondering how many other survivorship interests it or he, if it is an individual, might have bought out of bankruptcy. The Western District of Tennessee is only one of many districts and Tennessee is only one of many states that have a tenancy by the entirety and survivorship provision in their laws. Do you want to look into it?"

"Well, admittedly, you've got my curiosity up, but how is Worthmore or whoever going to rake in this $275,000. You've said that the interest isn't worth anything," said Watson.

"Unless the surviving spouse dies," said Carter.

"And?" replied Watson.

"She just did," said Manning.

"No shit!" exclaimed Watson.

"Yeah, no shit," replied Carter.

"How did she die? asked Watson.

"Well, that's another thing. She drowned. In a car accident. It's in your paper. Car went over the embankment on Ridgeway into Nonconnah the other night."

Chapter 22

Bob picked up the mail as usual from the mailbox and went through several of the envelopes. One was from Great Mortgage, which he immediately opened. He knew that his mortgage was current and he had had no problem with getting his mortgage loan reaffirmed following the bankruptcy, just as his lawyer had said. They were happy to help a good customer with such a fine payment record.

He looked at the letter quizzically as it stated "Congratulations!" As he read further, he read that his mortgage loan had been completely paid off and the company would be filing a Release Deed for their security on his house. He thought to himself, *What the hell?* I haven't paid off the mortgage. Then he saw another letter with an embossed *Worthmore Financial* and no return address. He opened it. It read:

Dear Sir: By registered Quit Claim Deed, filed under Register's No. 587423 in the office of the Shelby County Register, Chapter 7 Trustee, Robert Easton, conveyed all of his right, title and interest that he had as the Chapter 7 Trustee in your bankruptcy case No. BK 2018-5873, to Worthmore Financial. As a result of your wife's death, the interest that Worthmore purchased has become a fee simple interest, subject only to the first mortgage in favor of Great Mortgage Company of Minnesota, and the equity credit line you established with SunTrust Bank, both of which have been paid in full.

Therefore, you are hereby notified that Worthmore Financial now holds a clear title to your house at 6356 Old Oak Way, Memphis, Tennessee, 38119. This is your notice to vacate this property within 30 days of the date of this letter or you will be legally evicted. In such case, you will be responsible for all legal fees and costs that may be incurred by Worthmore in the proceeding if required to remove you and your belongings from the property.

Yours truly, Worthmore Financial

The letter was unsigned.

Bob thought he might have a heart attack. *What? How is this possible? My God, what else can happen to me, he thought, and who the hell was Worthmore Financial?*

Chapter 23

Tom Watson was a pretty good investigative reporter, or so he considered himself. The first thing he did was go to his own newspaper article on the death of Sally Conners. Not a whole lot of information, he thought, so he called the reporter that had written the article for the General News section.

"Agnes, this is Tom in Metro," he said, "Got a minute."

"Sure, Tom, as the kids say 'wassup?'" she said.

"I have an angle I am following up on the death of the woman who went into Nonconnah Creek just the other night," he said. "You wrote it up. Is there any follow-up on the story?"

"No, not really, Tom. No particular reason that I know of. It's a sad story all right. She was a mother of two and the police are not really sure why she went over the embankment. I just assumed it was a tragic accident and haven't gone farther with it. Should I?" she asked.

"I'm not sure," he replied. "I'm just doing some background. A lawyer contacted me and told me that as a result of her death, the family might lose their house. Something about her husband having filed bankruptcy six months ago and the Trustee selling the husband's survivorship interest to a Worthmore Financial, who no one has ever heard of."

"Really," said Agnes. "That puts a whole new light on this being a human-interest story."

"Yeah," said Tom. "I agree. See what you can find out from the police, will you? I'm trying to track down the financial company."

"You bet," she replied. "I'll find out if there is anyone investigating what happened and let you know. Thanks for the tip."

Agnes immediately called the East Precinct and asked to speak to whomever was investigating the auto accident that involved the woman going into the creek. She identified herself as a reporter following up on the previous story in the paper.

"That would be Lt. Martin, I think," came the reply from the desk sergeant. "Seems like I heard he was looking into the cause of the accident," he said. "Hang on, I'll buzz him."

"Martin," Detective Martin said as he picked up his phone.

"Agnes Stevens here, Lt. Have you got a minute to talk to me about the accident on Ridgeway the other night? The woman was drowned in her car."

"What's your interest in this?" replied Martin.

"I don't know, maybe minimal, but it's a human-interest story and I'm following up. She was only 43, married and had two children. I checked with the coroner's office and was told that other than drowning, they had no causation. No alcohol, no drugs. I mean, what makes a mother who was returning from grocery shopping go over an embankment if weather wasn't a causative factor? I've seen the detour and while it wasn't well lighted, it isn't hard to maneuver."

"It's under investigation," he replied unhelpfully.

"What's that mean?" she asked.

"It means that it's under investigation," he said and hung up on the reporter.

"Well, thanks a lot," she said.

Chapter 24

"Lt. Martin?" said the voice on the telephone.

"This is Martin. Who's this?"

"Danny over at latent prints. You gave me the cigarette butts on your investigation of the car crash."

"Oh, yeah, Danny. Got something?" Martin asked.

"Possibly. I was able to lift a bit of a fingerprint off each of the filters of the cigs. You want to run it through the index? It's not a great scrunch, but I would give it a 5 out of 10 for making a match if you can give me a print to match it with.

"I absolutely do. Get what you got to me pronto," said Martin. "And, thanks."

Chapter 25

Bob Conners came into Carter Manning's office and he was irate and combative, waving the letters he had just received from Great Mortgage, SunTrust and especially Worthmore Financial that gave him 30 days to get out of his house.

"What the bloody hell, Manning," he yelled. "Did you know about this? You told me that my marital interest was safe from any action by the Trustee, and now this Financial Company says they bought it from the Trustee and now that Sally is dead, they own the house and I have to get out!" Bob almost screamed.

"No, Mr. Conners," said Carter. "I did not know that the Trustee had sold the survivorship interest. I just found out about it myself and was going to contact you today. I am just as shocked as you are and have just spoken to the Chapter 7 Trustee about it."

"You know when we talked before the filing, I did tell you that your survivorship interest in property held by a husband and wife, the tenancy by the entirety, was a property right that passed to the Trustee in bankruptcy, but in all cases that I have handled, the Trustee has disclaimed that interest. To my knowledge, this is the only time that a Trustee has actually sold it, even though he legally can and legally someone can buy it. Without the death of the non-filing spouse, in this case, tragically your wife, this interest is virtually worthless," said Carter Manning apologetically.

"And this company can now put me out of my own house!" wailed Bob, almost in tears.

"You can challenge this in court," said Carter, "but if the Quit Claim Deed holds up as a valid transfer and the other prior secured debts on the property have been paid, then, yes, that purchaser would have fee simple title and can possess the property as the new owner. Since the first mortgage has been paid, as well as your equity credit line, perhaps this Worthmore Finance might be interested in giving you a new mortgage that may allow you to keep the house. I get the impression that it bought the Trustee's interest as a gamble, which, unfortunately and tragically, has paid off in its favor."

"Are you going to challenge this transfer?" said Bob.

"Yes," said Carter, "I will do that and I am also looking into this Worthmore Financial and have contacted a newspaper reporter that I know and he is looking into it as well. As far as I know right now, this company doesn't have an address other than a P.O. Box. Not even a website or telephone number in the phone book nor can I find any information about it on the internet. This is very strange to say the least."

"I've seen a copy of the Quit Claim Deed the Trustee signed," Carter continued, "and there is no indication it was prepared by an attorney, but it doesn't have to have been. That kind of deed is very simple and can be found in any real estate form book or book of legal forms. It only requires that the transferor's signature, that is the Chapter 7 Trustee in this case, be notarized. Pay the filing fee to get it registered in Shelby County, which is minimal, and the new owner is shown of record on the title, subject to any challenge to the title by a contesting party."

"Even more unusual," he continued, "is that no address is shown for the transferee, in this instance, Worthmore Financial. This is customary so the Clerk can mail a copy to the transferee or the attorney who might have prepared it, after registration, which means that it was a "walk-in" and "walk-out." Whoever took the deed to the Clerk's office waited for it to be recorded. A lawyer generally doesn't wait unless it is a special case to get a copy of a recorded deed that day. As I said, normally, the Clerk mails the recorded deed back to the address on the deed. They didn't do that here because there is no return address. I promise you I will look into it and am doing so."

Chapter 26

Tom Watson called Carter's office and asked to speak to him.

"Carter, this is Tom. I've been doing some leg work on this Worthmore Financial, and this company is what is known as a 'phantom'." It has no footprint to speak of. Reminds me of a washing machine for illegal cash, you know, connected to a foreign bank, like in Antigua, or someplace like that. Hard to trace. Not even sure it has an E.I. number, which it doesn't need I suppose if it has no employees and files no income tax return. It would have to have an E.I. if it has a bank account. With no E.I., it doesn't exist as far as the government is concerned. It isn't registered in Tennessee as a corporation according to the Secretary of State. In all likelihood, it is just a trade name invented by an individual to do business under. Any income reported would be in the name of the individual, if he or she reports it. What are we on to here?"

"Wow," said Carter. "I really don't know. Robbie Easton, the Chapter 7 Trustee, said he received a cashier's check with the Quit Claim Deed for the interest he sold to it."

"Where did the check come from, I mean, a cashier's check means that a bank provided it, right?" asked Tom.

"Don't know, but I can call and find out. Maybe Robbie made a copy of the check before cashing it. Can you plunk down $1,000 on a bank counter and ask for a cashier's check?" asked Carter.

"You know you can," replied Tom. The bank takes cash."

"Yeah, but normally, a bank won't do that unless it is for a customer that they know or maybe has an account with them," said Carter.

"Maybe they did know whoever got the check. The payee has to be named and the funds had to come from this Worthmore Financial in some form as the purchaser of the check, and, of course, in this case, it is also the buyer of the interest from the Trustee," said Tom.

"I'm going to call Robbie right now," said Carter.

Chapter 27

"You know what bothers me about this Mercedes," said Lt. Martin, "is why was it left in the ghetto for any number of gangsta's to strip, and more importantly, how did it get there? What happened to whoever drove it there and where did they go?"

"Someone wanted it to go away," said Brad Thompson, another detective in the squad. "They wanted it stolen because it was involved in an accident."

"Okay," replied Martin, "I'll buy that, but he or they couldn't have known it would wind up involving a death even if the driver panicked after the crash and took off. Kids might have freaked out, but they would have removed the fender and the rest of the body work, stripped it and left it without tires or anything else. But it wasn't touched."

"We need to see if anyone in the hood saw the car," said Thompson.

"Yeah, pull up the patrol for that night. I want to talk with them. They would know the area and there are a bunch of apartments on Georgia. Maybe someone saw something. We need to do a canvas," said Martin.

Chapter 28

Detective Martin received a call at his office.

"This is Officer Gaines, Lt., you wanted to talk to me?"

"Yes, Gaines, I'm investigating a death of a woman the other night on Ridgeway Road. I think that her car got hit by another car, specifically a Mercedes, that you correctly called in as stolen. I'm interested in anything you might know about the car being left on Georgia Avenue, which I understand is in your patrol area. Good call on the car, by the way," said Martin.

"Sure, Lt., what can I tell you," said the officer.

"I'm thinking that a car like that, left where it was, would have been a target for some of the bangers in the neighborhood and I'm wondering if anybody might have seen it being left where it was, and why it wasn't stripped," said Martin.

"That's easy," said Gaines. "The guys in the hood would have immediately thought it was a plant, you know, by us, just waiting to pounce on whoever came near it with a slim jim."

"Okay, that makes sense. Did you do any canvasing of the neighborhood, maybe someone saw something?" said Martin.

"Nah, Lt., there was no reason to," said Gaines. "How does this figure into whatever you are investigating?"

"I'm thinking," said Martin, "that this car was left by one or more persons expecting it to be trashed or stolen, which it already was, to dispose of it because it had been involved in a crash. That crash resulted in the death of a woman."

"Wouldn't know about that, L.T. Do you want me to ask around some of the homies to see if they saw anything? You know at that time of night, there are usually a lot of locals out and about."

"Yeah, Gaines, I would like for you to just ask if anyone saw who got out of the car when it was left," said Martin. "Can you do that and let me know?"

"Sure, Lt., I know almost all of the boys that live in the projects, especially on Georgia," replied Gaines.

"Thanks," said Martin. "If they thought it was a plant, I'm sure someone was watching to see who took the bait."

"I'll see what I can find out," said Gaines.

Chapter 29

"Robbie," asked Carter of the Chapter 7 Trustee, "Did you happen to make a copy of the cashier's check you received from Worthmore on the purchase of the Debtor's interest?"

"No, Carter," he said. "You can't make a copy of a cashier's check, Carter. It would void the check if you did that."

"Yeah, I hadn't thought about that," said Carter, "but did you keep a record of it otherwise?"

"Sure," he said. "I wrote down the particulars, number of the check, who was the purchaser, the date and all, and of course it was made payable to me as the Chapter 7 Trustee and the case number. All legit. The check came from SunTrust Bank and I deposited it in my escrow account for the case and when it cleared, I signed the Quit Claim Deed, got it notarized by our secretary and mailed it back in the envelope."

"I did check with Judge Chalmers to see if I needed to get a formal approval, and he said no, that it was part of administering the case, though he said he had never had a purchaser either when he was a trustee. Since I didn't have to make a motion, I didn't send out any notices. Maybe I should have. Damn, this is going to be a problem, isn't it?" said Easton.

"I don't know. Maybe. Can you send me the particulars on the check and the address of Worthmore, even if it is a P.O. Box? I want to check this out," said Carter.

Chapter 30

"Hey, Lt., this is Gaines. I did some asking around about the Mercedes that was left, and a sometime snitch I work with in the area, Tyrone, said that he saw the car. Not much happens on Georgia Avenue that Tyrone doesn't know about."

"And?" said Martin.

"Tyrone said he was across the street, and watched when the car came. Said it was going slow and since it was a big black Mercedes, which he don't see too often, he watched it. He said he then saw another car, a gray Chevy sedan, come up behind the Mercedes and that a large, heavy-set white dude got out of the Mercedes."

"That man got into the Chevy and they drove off. Tyrone said that they could have been cops, he didn't think so, but he wasn't sure. Said he figured that if they were, the Mercedes was bait and according to Tyrone, 'his momma didn't raise no dummy' and he wasn't about to go near it. He would just see if some dumbass tried to mess with it, but we came by and spotted it as stolen before anyone else could take a whack at it," said Gaines.

"Did you ask Tyrone if he could identify the man that got out of the car?" asked Lt. Martin.

"Yeah, I did," said Gaines, "since you said the car might be involved in a death case you were investigating, and he said he was pretty sure that he could. The guy was big, like I said, and Tyrone said he lit up a cigarette before getting into the other car, so he saw his face and that he was "big and ugly" and according to Tyrone, not someone to mess with."

Chapter 31

As soon as he got the print composite from Latent Prints, Lt. Martin, had what he hoped would be enough and ran it through all the data of TBI and the FBI. He didn't really expect that it would amount to anything, since it wasn't a full print, but he thought he might get lucky, and sure enough, he did.

"The sub's name is Lorenzo Constatine, nickname 'Big Connie' and he did 3-5 at Joliet some years back. Rap sheet connects him with the Carmine family in New Jersey, most likely a hit man, and said to be a capo, but he was never convicted of some of the stuff he might have been involved in. He was convicted of manslaughter that was knocked down from a first degree on a plea deal," said Danny in Latent Prints. "Bad dude, as they say."

"Does the FBI have any address on him?" asked Martin.

"Nothing recent, so I'm told," Danny said. He did the whole shtick so he doesn't or didn't have a parole officer to report to. As far as they know, he's in the wind."

"Well, he's in Memphis, now," said Martin, "and up to no good. We'll put out a BOLO on him and I will see if I can get a warrant. We can put him in the Mercedes with the cigarette butts, but there's no proof that he drove the

Conners' woman's car off the road. If we could prove that he did that purposely, it will be a murder charge, first degree. My bet is that he was hired to do it, but we don't have any motive or why anyone would hire him to kill a 43-year-old wife and mother of two children."

"Well, I hate to say this Lt, 'cause you are the detective, I'm not," said Danny, "but I've always heard that when a wife dies, the first suspect is the husband."

"Yeah, that's true," said Martin.

Chapter 32

While Lt. Martin didn't want to think that the husband had anything to do with his wife's death, he also knew that Danny was right and he needed to check out the relationship, good or bad, that Bob Conners had with his wife. The first thing to do was to find out more about Robert Conners.

That wasn't difficult to do. Conners was a chemical engineer with a local petrochemical company or had been for some 20 years or so. He learned that the company had been bought out by a Dallas oil company in a merger that resulted in a number of highly paid executives, of which Bob was one, getting eased out in a typical downsizing event that occurred after such a merger.

He also learned that this had left him unemployed in his chosen field and that he was employed part-time at Walmart. His wife had taken a job at FedEx and the loss of employment had left the family strapped. He learned that a Robert Conners had had to file a bankruptcy and that this man, husband of the woman who was killed, was one and the same.

Martin surmised that having had to file bankruptcy because he was broke meant that Conners would not have any money to hire a mafia type to kill his wife. Besides, what was the point? She had virtually no estate to speak of and the life insurance on her life he learned was minimal. Besides, he had met and talked with Conners and his gut told him that he was genuinely distraught over the death of his wife and just didn't seem the type to try to kill his wife. He would have to check out "the other woman," question, but he knew that was not a likely scenario. Conners wasn't that type either.

Why, he wondered, *would anyone want her dead?*

Chapter 33

"Lt. Martin?" said the desk sergeant. "There's a Carter Manning, an attorney, who has asked to speak to the officer that is investigating the death of the Conners woman, and I told him that was you. Can you take the call?"

"Yeah, Sarge, put him on," said Martin.

"Lt. Martin, I don't know whether to call you Detective or not, which do you prefer?" said Carter Manning.

"Actually, my position is Detective, my rank is Lieutenant, so please call me Detective. What can I do for you?" said Martin.

"Good, I am an attorney, and I handle a lot of bankruptcy matters here in Memphis. I was, or am, the attorney for my client, Bob Conners, whose wife, Sally, died in the automobile accident I'm told you are investigating. The reason I am calling is I have discovered some really strange things that are related to her death, or rather, to his bankruptcy. Do you have a minute to listen to me?" said Carter.

"Absolutely, what did you say your name was again?" said Martin. "Carter Manning. I'm getting the unsupported feeling that my client's wife's death was not an accident. About six months ago, my client filed a bankruptcy petition and in that petition he listed property owned by him and his wife that is worth a good bit of money. His wife did not file and that resulted in just his interest in the property coming into what we call the bankruptcy estate, or simply what he owned as assets."

"This interest in property owned by a husband and wife is known as a tenancy by the entirety, and what that means simply is both spouses own the property together and if one of them dies, then the surviving spouse becomes the sole owner of the property. Do you follow me so far?" asked Carter.

"Yes, sir, I do, and I did know that your client filed bankruptcy. I learned that in the course of my investigation," said Martin.

"Okay, that's good. Now here is the important part of what I am telling you," said Carter. "If, rather than dying, one of the spouses files a bankruptcy petition, then the interest that the spouse has in the property owned by them together, goes into the bankruptcy estate as an asset."

"And?" said Martin.

"And that interest is what is known in law as a survivorship interest and as it is technically and legally an asset, it passes to the Chapter 7 Trustee appointed to administer the bankruptcy."

"And?" said Martin again.

"And that interest is normally and usually not a salable asset and normally and usually the Chapter 7 Trustee disclaims to that survivorship interest because it is of no value, that is it does not provide any right to possession of the property with the other spouse, but, and this is the important part, it is a salable interest and someone can buy it if they want to take a gamble that the non-filing spouse will die before the spouse that filed bankruptcy. Are you getting the drift here?" said Carter.

"Maybe," said Martin. "Are you saying that whoever bought this survivor interest might become the owner of the property if the other spouse who didn't file bankruptcy dies before the other spouse?"

"Bingo. You have nailed it. Is it a gamble that the non-filing spouse will die so that the interest the person bought from the Trustee becomes the full ownership? Yes, it is, and I can't say how often, if ever, this has happened, but now it has!" said Carter.

"So did someone buy this 'survivorship interest' from the Chapter 7 Trustee?" asked Martin.

"Bingo again, Detective. A company called Worthmore Financial paid $1,000 to the Trustee and got that interest in a Quit Claim Deed that, with the death of my client's wife, becomes a full ownership of the property."

"Damn, that is motive!" said Martin.

"Motive for what, Detective? Are you saying that you have a suspicion that Mrs. Conners' death was not an accident?" said Carter.

"We need to meet, Mr. Manning," Martin said. "Can I come to your office and discuss this further?"

"Absolutely, Lt.," replied Carter. "And I can tell and show you that the amount of money paid to the Trustee was in the form of a cashier's check on behalf of Worthmore Financial."

"So?" said Martin.

"So, as far as I have been able to determine thus far, Worthmore Financial doesn't exist," said Carter.

"Can I come to your office?" said Martin.

"When?" Carter replied.

"Now," he replied.

Chapter 34

Carter Manning showed Lt. Martin the information he had gotten from Robbie Easton.

"This is good, especially the check number," said Martin, "but I'm not sure that it will add much to our evidence. You have said that the purchase of the survivorship interest was legal."

"Yes, it is, but what happened to Mrs. Conners, if she was murdered, is not. Wouldn't that be part of the chain of evidence if you can prove that her car was pushed off the road?" asked Carter.

"We can only think that is what happened," said Martin. "We have no proof. We do know and can prove that the Mercedes struck the Conners' car, but we don't have any proof that it was intentionally done or who was driving the car when it happened. We can, maybe, establish that a suspect we have identified, a Lorenzo Constatine, was in the Mercedes, and maybe was the man who left the car on Georgia Avenue in its damaged condition."

"I say 'maybe,' because all we have to put him in the car are two cigarette butts with partial prints that the lab was able to generate a print from. The technician said that he fused the two partials and that he would only give the print a 5 out of the 10 points that he would need to testify that the print was that of the suspect. Any attorney could challenge the print and the tech says he would have to say it wasn't a positive match," said Martin.

"What's more," he continued, "is we can't prove he drove the car or even stole the car, although it is likely he did. We have a witness that says he can identify the man getting out of the Mercedes because he lit a cigarette after he got out, and his physical size was distinctive. Constatine is a suspect because he has done prison time and is linked with a mafia family in New Jersey."

"So, can you find him and interrogate him? Maybe he would tell who hired him to kill Mrs. Conners," asked Carter.

"We are looking for him," replied Martin, "but he is probably no longer in Memphis, and his whereabouts are unknown. Besides, even if we were able to locate him and bring him in for questioning, if he is the thug we think he is and is connected, he wouldn't say a word. Ever heard of *omerta*?" asked Martin.

"Isn't that some kind of code of silence? Seems I have read that mafia folks don't talk," said Carter.

"Yeah, exactly that, plus having been in stir, he knows he doesn't have to say anything without a lawyer, plus we have no grounds to hold him. What's the charge, grand theft auto?" said Martin. "And there were no fingerprints in the car that would even support a warrant for his arrest."

"Worthmore Financial has a P.O. Box. Someone comes and gets mail," said Carter. "Could you or another detective sit on that box and see who would show up?"

"And do what? It isn't illegal to rent a Post Office Box and no, the MPD doesn't have the manpower to watch a P.O. Box. Not sure there is anything to be gained by that. You want to set up a satellite law office in the Post Office 24-7?" asked Martin.

"No, I guess that's not practical," replied Carter. "Still, you and I both know that someone facilitated this, what should we call it, not a scam, maybe a plot, to buy my client's survivorship interest and then have his wife killed to accelerate the possession of the property, and to make a profit as a result of it," said Carter. "Even if legal, its criminal."

"Agreed," said Martin. "Now prove it."

Chapter 35

"Mr. Conners is here, Mr. Manning. He would like to see you, but he doesn't have an appointment on my books," said Lisa, Carter's secretary.

"That's okay, Lisa. I will be glad to see him. Please hold my calls, said Carter.

"I thought you should know that my house has been sold. It didn't take long and my children and I are moving to Houston," said Bob Conners. "The real estate agent said that the buyers paid $330,000, which I guess is about right. She got a 6% commission, Worthmore Financial got $310,200, and I get nothing. I asked how my house could be sold without any signature from me and was told that all that was required was a Quit Claim Deed from Worthmore. The deed was signed by a Dominic Falucci on behalf of Worthmore. I guess now we know who Worthmore Financial is," said Bob bitterly.

"I am very sorry, Mr. Conners," said Carter.

"You can save the crocodile tears, Mr. Manning," Bob said bitterly. "Hey, I'm free of debt, isn't that what we all wanted from filing the bankruptcy? A 'fresh start' you said. Well, I'm getting that. So are my children. We're actually glad to get out of the house, too many memories."

"I understand. Did you get employment in Houston?" said Carter.

"Yes," said Bob. "I will be working for a petrochemical company using my knowledge. They know my history about having to file bankruptcy and have discounted that blemish on my record. I will be paid well and I intend to pay all of my debt even though I don't have to. I'm not a deadbeat, Mr. Manning. I had no choice or at least I thought I had no choice. We could have sold our house, paid our creditors and been okay. We could have 'survived' and I would still have my wife."

"I think about that every day, Mr. Conners," said Carter. "I am convinced that your wife was murdered, but we have no way of proving it and no one to prosecute. This man, Dominic Falucci, holds himself out as an investor, and his company, Worthmore Financial, is nothing but a shell. I have alerted the IRS about the facts of this case. If, as I suspect, he files no income tax return, or if he does file, in his own name, I am reasonably confident that he doesn't include all of his income, such as from the proceeds of the sale of your house. The IRS will get him on income tax evasion. You will have your pound of flesh one day."

Chapter 36

The two men met in the park. One of the men gave the other a manila envelope.

"Here's your Christmas present, Judge," one of them said.

"I don't want whatever is in that envelope, Dominic," was the reply. "What I told you was idle talk at a cocktail party. I know you either killed that poor woman or you hired someone to do it. Regardless, you are a monster, a killer and a criminal. I met you here today to tell you that to your face. If I could prove you did any of what happened or had any part in it, I would go to the F.B.I. and you would go to the gas chamber."

"I wouldn't do that, if I were you," Dominic Falucci said threateningly.

Chapter 37

Bankruptcy Judge Winston Dalton Chalmers was known for his punctuality. He got to his office every morning at eight o'clock to study his calendar for the morning court session and he stepped through the door to his courtroom every morning at 9:30 a.m. He expected all lawyers in his court to be equally as punctual. He would not abide any excuses and if lawyers had to be in state court at the same time, he expected them to come to his court and to make excuses about conflicts to the other judges. They were to be in his court.

Margaret Patterson, Judge Chalmers long time secretary, was also expected to be at her desk when he came in, and she was. Always, unless she was sick, which was not often. She had developed many of her Judge's mannerisms and seldom offered much in the way of a desk side manner to lawyers who wanted to see the Judge.

So, when her Judge did not come through the door at 8 a.m. as he had for twenty years, that was unusual to say the least. When he still had not arrived by 8:30, she began to feel a little concerned. While her Judge was in good health, being a Judge takes a toll on the strongest of healthy individuals, and she had noticed that lately he had seemed somewhat preoccupied. She knew he had something on his mind, but he didn't share, even with her, who was his confidant in many respects, as he was a widower and not one for idle chatter.

And, when he wasn't there at 9:29 to open court, she was very concerned. Her telephone calls to his home were not answered. She contacted the U. S. Marshall's office and asked if someone could be sent to his home as she was most distressed at an inability to contact him.

Judge Chalmers did not have a cell phone and woe to any lawyer whose cell phone went off in his courtroom. The sign outside the courtroom door was adamant in expressing *NO cellphones allowed.*

The lawyers waiting to hear and dispose of their matters were likewise fidgeting and wondering what might be going on. Margaret stepped into the courtroom to advise that the Judge had been "detained" and presumably would be there shortly.

U. S. Marshall Tony Brandon had been dispatched to the Judge's residence, which was a small condominium downtown that overlooked the river. It was gated, so he asked the guard had he seen the Judge this morning and when the question was answered in the negative, Tony asked the guard to show him to the Judge's condo and also to see if his car was still in the space assigned.

The guard did so and they found the Judge's car in his assigned space, which gave Tony some concern. After repeated rings on the bell and loud knocking, Tony asked the guard if there was a master key, and if so, as a U.S. Marshall, he was going to see if anything might be amiss since no one had been able to get in touch with him. The

Judge lived alone and the first thing that came into Brandon's thoughts was that the Judge might have had a heart attack or other physical event that might have disabled him.

A master key was obtained and Tony and the guard as a witness opened the door and called out:

"Judge Chalmers, it's Tony Brandon, U.S. Marshall. Are you all right?"

There was no answer so Tony stepped into the foyer and called again, with the same result. No answer.

Tony walked through the condo's living area and toward a bedroom. The bedroom door was open and there was the outline of a figure in the bed, still covered over with a blanket.

Tony tried again, saying, "Judge Chalmers, are you all right?" No answer.

As Tony approached the bed, with the guard just inside the bedroom door, he saw the blood on the pillow and a revolver on the floor. From looking at the figure, he could see the outline of a bullet hole in his head.

Judge Winston Dalton Chalmers was dead.

Chapter 38

The two detectives, Bailey and Albertson, called in from the Memphis Police Department, went into the Judge's condo after being called by the local officers as it appeared to be a homicide. The condominium had been taped off and secured as usual procedure required.

The coroner was present and had examined the body and the bullet hole in the right temple. There was a .38 caliber pistol by the side of the bed.

"So, what do we have, Doc?" asked Detective Bailey.

"Single gunshot to the right temple, death instantaneously, with the gun on the floor," replied the coroner. "Looks like a suicide."

"Find any kind of a note?" asked Detective Albertson.

"No, not that I have seen," replied the coroner, "but I have just been examining the body. His study or office is in the other bedroom. Been waiting for you fellows."

"I understand he was a Judge, is that right?" asked Bailey.

"So I was told," said the coroner. "A U.S. Marshall was dispatched to the residence when the Judge didn't come into his office at his usual time. He found the body along with the security guard who works the gate for the residents.

They had to use a master key to get into the place, but nothing has been disturbed or touched. It was a shock to both of them."

"Was he a federal judge, then?" asked Bailey. "Has the F.B.I. been notified?"

"Not sure about that," he replied, "but certainly the U.S. Marshall's Office is aware of this. Presumably, they would make that contact. I don't know," answered the coroner. "Not my area of expertise."

"Has the area been dusted for prints?" asked Albertson.

"No, not yet. It hasn't been determined that this is a crime scene yet. Could be a suicide. It happens," said the coroner.

"Hmmm, yeah," replied Bailey. "Who is someone we can talk to about his mental state, I mean someone who knew the judge?"

"Well, again, not my territory. He lived alone. A widower so I am told," replied the coroner, "but every Judge has a secretary and I assume some good friends."

"Well, let's just hope the feds want to take it over," said Bailey.

Chapter 39

The news about Judge Chalmers' untimely death spread quickly through the bankruptcy bar. Judge Chalmers' death had left a deep hole in the administration of bankruptcy cases, all of which would have to be re-assigned to the other judges for a disposition. For many lawyers, his death was quite a shock, and the question of whether he had committed suicide, and, if so, what would have been the motivating cause, was the conversation of almost every lawyer.

When Carter Manning heard the news, he was more than a little curious since Judge Chalmers had been the Bankruptcy Judge for his case involving the undetermined death of his client's wife. At least, it was undetermined in his mind. Just too many unresolved questions surrounding her death, if it was an accident.

Carter had kept in touch with Detective Martin, but the case had gone cold and there were no leads on the whereabouts of Constantine, nothing could be proven by the damage to the Mercedes and as far as either Manning or Martin were able to determine, there was nothing illegal about the sale of Conners' house to a fair market buyer for a fair market price. Carter had not been able to find out anything about Dominic Falucci or Worthmore Financial although he had tried, as had Tom Watson, Carter's contact at *The Commercial Appeal*.

So when the news about the Judge's death and supposed suicide became front page news, Carter called Martin.

"Detective Martin, this is Carter Manning. Have you seen the newspaper article in the paper today about the death of Bankruptcy Judge Chalmers?"

"Can't say I have, Mr. Manning," replied Martin. "Is this something that has to do with your client's bankruptcy case? Seems there are some strange doings over there recently."

"I can't say whether it has any connection or not," said Carter, "but he was the Bankruptcy Judge that oversaw the Conners' case. The article indicates his death was a suicide, and, of course, this case was just one of hundreds that the Judge had been assigned. I just thought you might like to have this bit of information."

"Well, sure," Martin said. "Can't always tell."

"The article says that the case has been assigned to two of your fellow detectives, Albertson and Bailey. Do you know them pretty well?" asked Carter.

"Yeah, they are good detectives," replied Martin. "I can ask them what it looks like to them. I'll get back to you."

Chapter 40

Albertson and Bailey, as detectives go, were good detectives, but they didn't bother to look beyond what appeared to them to be the obvious, which in this case was a suicide. No sign of forced entry into the Judge's condo, gun by the side of the bed and nothing to indicate foul play. The gun was a .38 caliber and while not registered to the Judge, it was an older pistol that he might have had in his possession for 40 years and could not be traced.

A flaw in the suicide story was the lack of a note, but they knew that not every suicide case left a note. From a cursory canvass of the neighbors, they found nothing to indicate that the Judge had had any visitors of a suspicious nature. He normally kept to himself and was pretty much an ideal neighbor, quiet and scholarly in nature. They found nothing to warrant much of a further investigation.

As the Judge was a federal Judge, they had an obligation to contact the U.S. Attorney and share what their investigation had revealed, which was not much. Although the F.B.I. would have a concurrent jurisdiction to investigate, Albertson and Bailey were only too happy to turn it over to the "Feds" and move on. They did contact the Judge's secretary and asked if he had been depressed over anything or if she might have any clue as to why he might take his own life. She did not and was very distressed over his death. She had been his secretary and confidant for many years and felt that she would know if anything was really bothering him.

So when Detective Harvey Martin called on Albertson for some information about the investigation, he received a rather cold shoulder should he want to come back behind them and snoop around in what they had determined was a suicide. They knew Martin's reputation in the department as a loner and one who often found clues that sometimes led him to a different conclusion, to the chagrin of the other detectives.

"It's a suicide, plain and simple," said Albertson. "You never know what's going through a jumper's mind, Martin, and no, we haven't investigated it as anything else. You're always trying to find something that doesn't exist, so butt out."

"Okay, so you shouldn't have any objection to my looking at the file for Christ's sake," said Martin. "I've got this lawyer on my back and he thinks the Judge's death may have some connection to a case he had recently where his client's wife drowned in an auto accident."

"So what's the connection?" asked Albertson.

"Not sure. May not be any. I'm not going to step on your toes," replied Martin.

"Sure, Martin, knock yourself out, and say hello to the Feds while you're at it. They're sniffing around as well, and Martin, screw you," said Albertson.

Chapter 41

Detective Martin secured the file and began to go through it. The coroner's report was routine in its cause of death by a single gunshot to the right temple by a .38 caliber bullet, which was recovered and tested. The bullet came from the gun found on the floor of the scene and death was instantaneous.

Martin examined the pictures of the bedroom, body in the bed and gun on the floor. No sign of any struggle, forced entry or anything else to indicate anything of a criminal nature. He thought just perhaps Albertson and Bailey were right in their conclusion of a suicide, but he was too good of a detective and he trusted his gut, so he would start at the beginning, which meant a trip to the Judge's condo.

Because the Judge's death was not considered to be a crime at this point, no tape was over the door. The security guard called the manager of the complex who came and met Martin to let him in. The manager asked him not to disturb any of the Judge's personal books or papers as he had just received a call from the F.B.I. and that agents were also wanting to look around and would be there shortly. Martin said he wouldn't be long.

As Martin looked around the living quarters, he could see that the Judge was a neat resident and may presumably have had a housekeeper come in from time to time. He made a mental note to ask about that and to get a name if there was one.

The living area looked out over a small patio area behind glass doors, which led to an impressive view of the Mississippi River and down to the Riverside Trail for bikers and those who walked the trail. Martin noted that the overlook had a railing and that the trail was maybe about twenty feet down from the rail, again, presumably, for safety. He made another mental note to go down to the trail and observe whether a person could scale the grade and get on the balcony. He remembered, however, that the lab found no footprints or mud on the carpet inside the glass partition, but made another mental note to check that as well.

As he went through the rest of the condo, he could see that one of the rooms had a desk, chair, a computer and shelves of books. Some papers were on the desk, which he glanced over without disturbing them, and determined that it was pretty obviously the Judge' study where he reviewed and wrote some opinions for law cases and the like. Nothing seemed to him to be disturbed or scattered and law books were beside the computer. There was also a printer connected to the computer and again, nothing out of the ordinary.

Martin stood in the doorway of the Judge's bedroom and compared it to the pictures in the case file that he had copied. The blood stain on the sheets and pillow case had not been disturbed except during the removal of the body. There was a chalk outline of the gun that had been found on the floor next to the bed. He saw no other outlines on the floor and the carpet was a usual short pile.

The table by the bed had a lamp and an alarm clock, again nothing disturbed. He noted the time on the clock when the pictures were taken by the lab. The file had indicated that the Judge's body was not discovered until the U.S. Marshall and the security gate guard had entered the condo at approximately 10:00 a.m.

The coroner's report indicated that the time of death was between 10:00 p.m. and 4:00 a.m. Although the Judge's condo was one of several in a row which overlooked the river, their canvass of the neighbors did not indicate that any of them had heard a shot during that time period. As close as the condos were to one another, Martin thought that was strange since a .38 caliber pistol makes a loud report when fired.

He quickly went through the rest of the condo, looked into the kitchen, which was neatly arranged, a few closets of no great interest and was about to walk out of the condo when a man and a woman met him at the door. They were surprised at seeing anyone in the condo and after announcing "Federal Agents" and drawing their weapons, Martin explained he was a Detective with the Memphis Police Department and things calmed down a bit.

"What are you doing here, Detective Martin?" asked one of the agents.

"I could ask you the same thing," replied Martin. "What does the F.B.I. have to do with a death ruled as a suicide?"

"Judge Chalmers was a United States Bankruptcy Judge," replied the woman, "and that makes him a federal officer. We have the right and the duty to investigate his death. That's what we are doing here," she said haughtily. "Now what are you doing here, Detective?"

"The same as you," replied Martin defensively. "A death in the City of Memphis is a concern until it has been definitively ruled as a suicide and not a homicide. This judge's death may have a connection with another case I have open.

"And what is that case?" came the reply.

"If it becomes relevant," Martin replied, "I will let you know."

Chapter 42

Before Martin left the condos, he went down and around to get to the river trail. From a position down from the railing of the Judge's condo, he looked up and could see it was about twenty to twenty-five feet on a steep grade. The overlook to the river jutted out over the grade. He thought that while it might be difficult to climb up to the overlook, it wasn't impossible. He thought a rope ladder could be tossed over the railing and could be climbed. It made him wonder if the Judge kept the glass doors to the patio locked. He wondered if Albertson and Bailey had bothered to check the glass door since there was no evidence of a forced entry through the front door of the condo.

The next stop was the U.S. Bankruptcy Court building. He wanted to talk to the Judge's long-time secretary, Margaret Patterson. He had read the interview transcript of her by Albertson and Bailey, but there was one question he wanted to know the answer to that was not in that transcript and she would be the one person who would know.

"Mrs. Patterson, I am Detective Harvey Martin. We spoke on the telephone," said Martin. "Thank you for allowing me to come talk with you. I know you are distressed over the Judge's death and I will be brief."

"I have already told the other officers I talked with what I know of about that morning. The Judge was always very punctual and when he didn't come in at his usual time, when we meet to go over his cases for the morning, I just knew something was wrong. Especially when he didn't call and I couldn't reach him at home. He always let me know if for any reason he would be late, I mean, a doctor's appointment or something," said Mrs. Patterson. "When he wasn't here for court at 9:30, that's when I called the Marshall's office."

"Yes, Ma'am," replied Martin. "I read the transcript, but you more than anyone, perhaps, would know if anything had been bothering the Judge, I mean, maybe a difficult case or something that had happened that might have been the reason for his taking his life."

"No," she replied. "Of course, he always took every case as being important, as it is, or was, to the Debtors that came before him. Being a Bankruptcy Judge is very stressful, Detective."

"The reason I am asking is that I am aware of a specific case about six months ago involving a man named Conners, whose wife died recently. Do you know of this case?" Martin asked.

"Is this the one where there was a purchase of the Trustee's survivorship interest?" she asked.

"Yes," he replied. "With the death of the man's wife, the family lost their house. It was in the paper recently, at least the death of the wife was. She lost control of her car and went over an embankment into Nonconnah Creek and drowned."

"Oh, yes, I do remember that one," she said, "and to be frank, her death was very disturbing to him. Do you think that that case has anything to do with his taking his life?"

"I don't know. Do you?" he replied.

"Oh, surely not. I mean, it was tragic what happened, but it was an accident, wasn't it?" she asked.

"That is still under investigation, that is all I can tell you right now. It certainly appears to have been an accident, but there was another car involved, and while we can't prove it, the other car may have been the reason that the Conners woman lost control of her car. We can't say it was intentional, but there are some odd issues that simply don't add up, and now Judge Chalmers, who was the judge on the Conners' case, has taken his life."

"Oh, my God," she said.

"So you don't think that Judge Chalmers' concern over what happened caused him to go into such a depressed state that he would have committed suicide?" asked Martin.

"No, I saw no evidence of any change in his demeanor or mental condition. Certainly not to that extent, anyway," she replied. "Like I said, her death distressed him."

"One other question, please. Was the Judge right-handed or left-handed?" Martin asked.

"He was left-handed," she replied. "Why do you ask?"

"Judge Chalmers died from a bullet fired into his right temple. That would be unusual for a left-handed man to use his right hand," he said.

Chapter 43

While Judge Chalmers' death was quietly being investigated by both the F.B.I. and Detective Martin, his daughter who lived in New York came to Memphis to make funeral arrangements. Patsy Chalmers was his only heir and she had been advised by her father that she was to be the Executrix of his estate. As such, she had a copy of his Last Will and Testament and knew that the original was kept in a safe deposit box at First Tennessee Bank. She had also been advised that the key to the safe deposit box was in his office desk at the bankruptcy court building and she was very familiar with Margaret and her relationship to her father. Consequently, when she came to his office to retrieve the key, both she and Margaret were comfortable in going through the Judge's desk drawers to locate the key, which they did, just as he had instructed.

Because she had the key to the safe deposit box, the teller had no reason to question her right to entry, especially since she was on the list of persons entitled to entry as provided by her father. When she opened the box, she found the original Will as expected, the title papers to the condo, some gold coins and other personal papers relating to his marriage to his wife. All of this was to be anticipated to be in an orderly fashion, much like her father lived.

She also found an envelope that her father had addressed "To be opened in the event of my death," which she assumed would have instructions for his funeral arrangements. When she opened it, however, it contained no instructions as expected, but rather a most disturbing recitation:

"When this envelope is opened, I will be dead. I am writing this because my death may, or may not, have been as a result of any medical condition that I have, or be diagnosed to have had, that resulted in my death."

"I say that my death may not have been as a result of any medical condition, because I have a distinct fear that it may be because I have been murdered," Patsy gasped when she read this.

"That being said, whoever is in possession of this letter, I want you to advise the appropriate authorities so my death can be investigated if there is a lack of medical certainty that it was as a result of natural causes."

"I have done nothing in my career as a lawyer or a Bankruptcy Judge that may be considered criminal. I have, however, had associations with some people who may be guilty of criminal acts. I cannot be certain of this, nor can I establish any proof that would lead to a conviction in a court of law for any act that may have been committed."

"Regardless, I feel that my life has been threatened because of what I believe to be true, and, if so, a murder has been committed. This would be the murder of a woman

named Sally Conners, which occurred a few days prior to the date of this writing."

"I believe that although her death was attributed to an automobile accident as reported in The Commercial Appeal recently, the accident was purposely caused in order to cause her death so that property owned by her and her husband could be confiscated and sold for financial profit. The manner in which this property was confiscated, while lawful in form, was not lawful if her life was taken solely to accelerate that confiscation."

"I am referring to what is known in law as a 'right of survivorship' which exists between a husband and wife when property is owned by them. Simply put, the survivor of them, in the event of death, becomes the sole owner of property they owned together as husband and wife."

"Ordinarily, this property relationship is inviolate, but if one of the married persons files a bankruptcy, the existence of the property ownership of that person becomes a property right that passes to a trustee in bankruptcy. This is the "right of survivorship" and is a salable asset of the bankrupt."

"In a recent case filed by a Robert Conners that came before me as a Chapter 7, that right of survivorship was sold by the Trustee assigned to the case to an entity known as Worthmore Financial. Worthmore Financial is solely owned by a man I know as Dominic Falucci."

"I believe that this man purposely caused the death of Mr. Conners' wife, though, as I have said, I have no proof. I do not know how Mr. Falucci learned of the legal relationship which is created when a husband and wife buy property and title this property as "tenants by the entirety," *but he inquired of me specific information about the right of survivorship one evening at a reception I attended, and, unwittingly, I explained how that "right of survivorship" could be sold in a bankruptcy context."*

"I regret doing this. I later learned that Mr. Falucci did, in fact, buy this right in the Conners case. I thought nothing about it at the time, thinking he was throwing his money away. I am now afraid that this was a concocted plan which, after the wife's death, led to the legal confiscation of the Conners' home place and the subsequent sale, resulting in a 'windfall' of over $275,000 or more."

"I confronted Mr. Falucci with my suspicions, and he made a threat against me. Though he knows that nothing can be proven and that what was done in the purchase and sale was legal, I am in fear of my life as a result of his threat. If he killed, or was responsible in some way for the death of Conners' wife, I have not the slightest doubt that he would not hesitate to silence any allegation of his crime from me."

"Therefore, while it may not do any good, I request that anything that can be done by local, state or federal authorities to determine whether Dominic Falucci is guilty of the murder of Sally Conners be instituted."

The letter was signed and dated by Judge Chalmers.

Chapter 44

Patsy Chalmers sat stunned as she read the letter from her father, wondering what she should do. She gathered up the original Will and what other documents she thought she might need for the probate of his estate, made an inventory of the other items in the lock box and returned the box to its location in the vault room. When she left the bank, she knew what she needed to do.

"Margaret, this is Patsy," she said. "Do you have some time to talk? I need to show you something from Dad that I found in his lockbox at the bank. Maybe you can tell me what I should do."

Margaret was just as stunned as Patsy was when she read the letter. They were both aghast at its content and what it might mean relative to the Judge's death.

"Do you think Dad might have been murdered?" asked Patsy. "This letter seems to say that he thought it was a possibility."

"I don't know, Patsy, but I do know what we need to do with this letter. I talked to a Detective from the Memphis Police Department and he told me things that are relevant to the case mentioned by your father in this letter. I have his card here and we can call him. He needs to see this," Margaret said.

Patsy took the card and went back into her father's office to make the call.

"Harvey Martin," he answered, when he got the call.

"Detective Martin, this is Patsy Chalmers. We have not met, but I got your card from Margaret Patterson, whom you talked with recently. I am Judge Chalmers daughter. I live in New York, but came here to Memphis as soon as I was notified of Dad's death."

"Yes, Miss Chalmers," said Martin. "I'm very sorry for your loss."

"Detective, I'm calling you because of a letter I found in my father's lock box at the bank. I went there to get his Will as I am the Executrix of his estate appointed in that Will. Margaret said that you were doing an investigation about a woman who drowned in a car accident and that you weren't sure it was an accident," Patsy said.

"Well, yes," said Martin, "the case is still open to that extent, but it has not been determined to be a homicide."

"This letter from my dad has on the envelope: 'To be opened in the event of my death,'" said Patsy, "and I think it is relevant to your investigation. Dad says he is sure that her death was not an accident, and I think that you will want to read it."

"Of course, Miss Chalmers, thank you for calling me about it," said Martin. "I would very much like to read it. Can we meet someplace?"

"I am at my dad's office and I want to give you the original. We can make any number of copies here that you may need, but I want to make sure that this original is

122

preserved as my father wants an investigation," Patsy said. "Can you come here and take custody of it?"

"I will be there in twenty minutes," he replied.

Chapter 45

When Detective Harvey Martin read the letter from the Judge, he felt that this was the piece missing from his case, but again, the Judge offered no proof. He took an affidavit from Patsy Chalmers as to when and where the document was found and that it was all in the Judge's handwriting. He noted the left slant of the writing of a left-handed man, and knew then he would be returning to the Judge's condo and the river trail beneath the overlook. In his opinion, it was sufficient to open a murder book in both cases.

Martin had Margaret make several copies of the letter and the affidavit and gave a signed receipt to the Judge's daughter, taking custody of the original of the document as she requested.

When he got back to his office, he pulled out the cards of the F.B.I. Agents that they had given him when they met at the condo, and placed a call directly to Agent Simon.

"Special Agent Simon," she answered promptly and crisply.

"Agent Simon, this is Detective Harvey Martin. We met at the condo residence of Judge Chalmers."

"Yes, Detective," she said coolly. "I remember."

"Well, I told you that I would call and discuss this other case I still have open involving the death of a woman if I thought it had any relevance to the Judge's death," he said.

"And?" she replied.

"We need to talk," Martin said. "I have something I want to show you. It's relevant."

Chapter 46

Special Agent Simon was a raven-haired beauty, but she was all business when she met with Detective Harvey Martin in her office.

"So, Detective, you said you had something to show me that is related to the Judge's death?" she asked.

"Yeah, I do. This is a letter written by the Judge before his death and left in his lock box at the bank. His daughter found it and has given it to me. You need to read it," said Martin.

Agent Simon took the copy of the letter and read it. She then asked of Martin, "What do you know about this Dominic Falucci?"

"Actually, nothing," he replied. "I thought you might have some information about him. I get the impression that he is connected. Isn't that your area?"

"I can do some background on him, but right off hand he doesn't sound familiar," she replied.

"I have a thought that he might be with the Carmine family of New Jersey. You know of them, right? he asked.

"Yes," she replied. "But what is the connection, no pun intended."

"We believe that a Lorenzo Constatine may have been called in to do a hit number on the Conners woman by Falucci, but we have absolutely no evidence. He may or may not be connected with the Carmine family, but he has a record," he said.

"Why do you think Falucci hired him?" she asked.

"Because we believe that Falucci hatched a plot to pick up some easy cash based on a legal purchase of what the lawyers tell me is a 'right of survivorship.'"

"How does that work?" she asked.

"The simplest explanation is, so I understand it, is that anyone can buy an interest in real property from a Bankruptcy Trustee that is owned by a married couple if only one of them files a bankruptcy petition and the property is worth a lot of money. If the non-filing spouse dies, then that purchaser gets the property. It's a gamble, and can take some time for it to pay off, if it ever does, but not if you knock off the surviving spouse. That speeds up the process. Otherwise, the purchaser has to wait and see if his gamble pays off, which might be years, or if the other spouse dies, the purchaser gets nothing and he has wasted his money."

"And that's legal?" she asked.

"It is, as long as you don't commit murder by killing the surviving spouse," he replied.

"So why do you think this has anything to do with the Judge's death?" she asked.

"It may, or it may not," came Martin's reply. "But obviously the Judge thought this Dominic Falucci fellow was capable of speeding up the process of collecting on his purchase. Otherwise, he wouldn't have written this letter asking for an investigation of his death, if he died of unknown cause."

"So you think the Judge was murdered?" Simon asked.

"Not only the Judge, but the woman who was the surviving spouse in this bankruptcy case," he replied. "For it to work like it did, she had to die, and the Judge knew all about it with her death once she died. He believed, obviously, that Falucci killed her or had her killed."

"And Falucci knew that the Judge knew, even though there is no proof, and he didn't want to take the chance that the Judge would blow the whistle on him?" she added.

"That's my conclusion, I just can't prove it."

"How did the wife die?" Simon asked.

"Her car went over an embankment into Nonconnah Creek. I believe that her car was forced over by another car. We have the car that collided with her car, and there is no question that the collision was the cause of the Conners woman losing control of her car, but we don't have the driver," Martin said. "And we can't connect Falucci with either of the deaths."

"Do you have anything?" she asked.

"Only the possible fingerprint of Lorenzo Constatine found on cigarette butts in the Mercedes, which is the car that collided with the Conners' woman's car. No proof that would stand up in court, even if we can locate him, which, right now we can't. And there is no connection with Falucci and Constatine that we know of."

"And right now, the Judge's death is ruled as a suicide," she replied.

"Yeah. How about that," Martin said.

"Interesting," was her reply.

128

Chapter 47

Agent Simon said that she would see what she could find out about Falucci and Constatine and let Martin know. She was more inclined to work with him now that she understood how the two cases might be connected.

In the meantime, Martin went back to the Judge's condominium complex and the river walk trail that ran beneath the condos overlooks. He wanted to rule out the possibility of someone being able to climb the slope enough to get onto the railing and the patio area of the Judge's apartment. The glass doors were an easy access to the apartment, especially if they were not locked. While he thought he couldn't physically climb it, a younger and more agile man could.

Martin also followed up on his mental note about a housekeeper. In fact, the Judge did have a housekeeper that came in twice a week, according to the security guard at the gate. Her name was Maria Valdez and she worked for many of the residents in the condo community and had done so for years. She was completely trustworthy according to the other residents that employed her. Martin had no trouble in connecting with her to ask a few questions.

"Maria," he asked, "did the Judge have any people come around his place when you were there that were, you know, questionable or that were asking questions about him?"

"No, *Señor* Martin," she replied. "The Judge kept to himself and I never saw any of his visitors. Of course, I was generally gone before he came home."

"Did he lock his doors on a regular basis, if you know?"

"Yes, *Señor*. I always had Raymond, the security guard, let me in. Some of my employers, they give me keys, but not the Judge," she said.

"What about the glass doors to the patio? Did he keep those locked as well?" he asked.

"Well, no, *Señor*," Maria replied. "I would sometimes go out on the patio and those doors were not locked. It is a long way down the slope from the railing. It is not likely anyone would try to get in the apartment by climbing up from the river trail. Very difficult."

"And did anyone come to the apartment while you were there, maybe a repairman or someone like that."

"I only let in those persons who had jobs to do," she said. "The Judge he has trees in his backyard and the tree man he comes and prunes the fruit trees. The Judge is very proud of his peach tree and his apple tree. They produce much fruit. The only other man is the bug man. He comes into spray for bugs and ants. He comes once a month."

"And did anyone come this past month?" he asked.

"Yes, *Señor*. The bug man come and sprayed throughout the apartment. He actually come twice this month," she said. "I thought Judge have problem that he come twice."

"Was this the regular man you know?" Martin asked.

"Well, no, *Señor*. This different man," she said. "But he say that he supposed to spray, so I let him in."

"Same company?" he asked.

"Si, *Señor*, same company, different man," she replied.

"Maria, do you know if the Judge had a gun, a pistol of any kind in the apartment?"

"No, *Señor*. I not know about that. I only clean tops of tables and kitchen, change sheets and do laundry. I never see any gun."

"Okay, Maria. Thank you," he said.

Chapter 48

Detective Martin called Patsy Chalmers.

"Miss Chalmers, this is Detective Martin. Do you have a minute to answer a few questions?"

"Of course, Detective. What do you want to know?" she replied.

"Do you know where your father might have gotten the gun? Did you know he had one?" he asked.

"No, Detective. I really don't. He never showed it to me," she replied. "But, come to think of it, he did say one time that he was qualified to shoot a pistol. Seems like the F.B.I or some agency wanted him to be qualified for self-protection. I really don't know," she replied.

"Did you talk with him recently; I mean before his death? Did he seem disturbed or upset about anything? Anything at all that you can think of that might have caused him to take his life?" Martin asked.

"Yes, we talked often, and, yes, I did talk with him just a few days before, but he was his usual self. I don't know of anything that was on his mind or that would make him do this," she said softly. "I'm just at a complete loss."

"Okay, but you say he mentioned that he was qualified to shoot a pistol, so is it likely that he might have had one, maybe an old pistol that he had inherited from his father?" asked Martin.

"Again," she replied, "I really don't know. My grandfather was a shop keeper during the depression years and he might very well have had a gun for his own protection, you know, in case of an attempted robbery or something. It's certainly possible that my father got it from him."

"Okay, thank you, Miss Chalmers. I hope I won't have to bother you again."

"Call me anytime, Detective. I want to know what happened," she said tearfully.

Chapter 49

"You're really good. The paper says it was a suicide," said the voice on the telephone.

"You get what you pay for," said the other man. "Piece of cake. Found his own gun and the glass door on the patio was unlocked. Hardest thing was to climb up the trees to the overlook. The railing helped."

"How did you find his gun?" the voice asked.

"Got lucky on that. Went in as a pesticide man hired to do a spray. Used that before. Cleaning woman let me in. Gun was in his bedside table drawer. An old .38 revolver. Just where you would think a Judge would have a weapon if he had one. Most judges either carry one or have one close by," said the man. "He never checked the drawer or he would have seen it was missing after I took it. Sound sleeper. Never woke up. I used a baggie for the GSR and rubbed his hand with it. Guarantees a suicide if the cops find gunshot residue," he said.

"You did good. I'll let it be known," said the voice.

Chapter 50

One Week Later

The delivery man that came to the building on White Station Road was dressed like a UPS employee in his brown uniform and cap. He had a large manila envelope under his arm and a clipboard. He knocked on the door that the building manager said was the office of Worthmore Financial. Dominic Falucci was inside and answered the knock.

"Yes, who is it?" he said.

"UPS. I have a certified delivery for a Dominic Falucci," came the reply. "The building manager says this is his office."

"Just leave it at the door," Falucci replied.

"I'm sorry, sir. I have to get a signature for a certified delivery," he answered.

"Okay, just a minute," was the reply.

Dominic Falucci reached into his desk drawer and withdrew a snub nosed .38 caliber automatic pistol and put it in the small of his back. He opened the door and observed that the delivery man had a large envelope and a clipboard.

"Can you sign for Mr. Falucci?" the delivery man asked.

"I'm Falucci. I will sign," he replied. "What is it?"

"I really don't know, sir," as he handed Falucci the envelope and the clipboard, taking up both of Falucci's hands to hold the envelope and clipboard.

When he did, the delivery man produced a small caliber pistol with a silencer and fired two shots, one to Falucci's chest and the other to his head. Phhtt. Phhtt. Falucci was killed instantly and fell to the floor.

The delivery man picked up the envelope and the clipboard and closed the door to Falucci's office with a gloved hand and left the building.

It would be days before his body would be found.

Chapter 51

As soon as Detective Martin got word about the finding of Dominic Falucci's body, he called Agent Simon. She answered his call.

"Special Agent Simon."

Martin said, "Agent Simon, this is Harvey Martin. I hope you remember me. I have some news about the case we are working on, at least I still am. I don't know whether you are or not."

"Yes, Detective Martin," she said, "I'm still working on it if you mean the death of Judge Chalmers. That's my principal jurisdiction. The Conners case, not so much."

"Well," he said, "this may change your thoughts about whether the two are connected."

"How so?" she answered.

"You remember we talked about the man who purchased the Conners' survivorship, Dominic Falucci, and then actually got the house? Bought it out of bankruptcy?"

"Yes," she said, "you thought he might have a mafia relationship with the Carmine family."

"Right," Martin continued. "Well, they just found his body in his office. He'd been shot a couple of days ago. The coroner is doing the post mortem now."

"Falucci is dead?" she said with surprise in her voice.

"Oh, yeah. He's dead alright," Martin said. "Looks like a professional hit. One to the chest and a second to his forehead."

"And you think Falucci is the one that was responsible for the Judge's death, if it wasn't a suicide?"

"Yes. Can't prove it yet, but this is not just a coincidence. Someone made the decision that Falucci was a threat or knew too much, not sure which," said Martin.

"There are just too many bodies turning up. Or it could have been some type of revenge killing. Falucci wasn't a boy scout."

She said, "I did do some background check on him with his family connections, and you are right about the Carmine family. Seems Dominic was the nephew of Vito Carmine, head of the family in New Jersey. According to what I have been able to find out, his uncle wasn't too happy with Dominic. It seems he went rogue and some of his ideas didn't sit well with Vito."

"Well, killing a federal judge would seem to be a pretty poor idea, if he did," said Martin.

"If he did," she said.

"So we have a lot of questions and no answers," he said.

"Do you think it could have been a revenge killing?" she asked. "Does he have enough enemies that would want to see him dead?"

"Don't know about that," he said, "but they found a gun on the floor of the office. Evidently, he was careful about who he opened the door to."

"Perhaps he wasn't so careful this time," she said.

"Yeah, seems that way," Martin said.

Chapter 52

With the killing of Falucci, Detective Martin was now of the opinion that all of these deaths, Sally Conners, Judge Chalmers and now Falucci, were connected. He also thought that the Judge's death was not a suicide, despite the conclusion of Albertson and Bailey that it was and the case was closed as far as they were concerned. It just didn't sit right with Martin, however, especially a left-handed man shooting himself in the head on his right side.

Also, there appeared to be no reason for him to take his life.

According to his secretary and his daughter, he was not greatly disturbed about anything, but then there was his letter. The thought of someone, namely Falucci, making him think his life was in danger should have been enough for him to show some stress. Perhaps that is why he had the pistol by his bed, if it was his.

Martin thought to himself, *When there's nothing there, we're not looking hard enough.*

He returned to the river walk below the Judge's condo, this time with some powerful binoculars. There were several trees on the slope that could provide hand and foot holds to an agile person to get up on the terrace. He scanned the branches that would seem to be the most likely way of scaling the slope, if one wanted to do that, and he saw what he was looking for: A broken branch.

"Damn, I knew it," he said to no one.

Chapter 53

Lorenzo Constatine entered the plush den of Vito Carmine's home.

"Godfather," said Constatine to Vito Carmine, "I have just received news that your nephew, Dominic, was found dead in his office in Memphis."

"Dominic, dead?" Vito responded in shock.

"Yes, Godfather," said Constatine without emotion.

"What do you know about his death?" asked Vito.

"Very little, Godfather. He was found in his office and it is said that he had two gunshot wounds, one to his chest and the other to his forehead. He had been dead a couple of days before they found his body. The smell, you know."

"In Memphis? So that's where he went to," said Vito.

"Yes, Godfather. He contacted me about three weeks ago. Said he wanted me to do a little job for him down there and to bring someone I trusted. Rocco and me went down to Memphis to meet with him and he explained what he wanted done. He didn't say why, but he wanted a woman killed and he wanted it to look like an accident."

"We identified her from an address Dominic had and we followed her routine. She went to a grocery store every so often from her home and the route she took went over a small river where they were building a bridge. There was a detour road and a steep embankment. We decided that we could push her car over the embankment and she would most likely drown in the river."

"And did you do this?" asked Vito.

"Yes, Godfather. The job went smoothly. The woman drowned and it was considered an accident. We left the car that we had used on a Memphis street and came back here. There is nothing to trace us. We were very careful and wiped off any prints on the car we stole, if there were any."

"When was this?" Vito asked.

"It has been several weeks ago," Constatine answered.

"And you don't know why he wanted this woman killed?" asked Vito.

"No, Godfather, and we didn't ask. We received payment as promised, but we had no contact with him," he said. "She was just a housewife. As far as we know, he had no relationship with her."

"This was another one of his schemes!" Vito said in disgust. "Now he is dead! He always was a damn fool. If he had just come to work for the family, he would be alive."

"Yes, Godfather," Constatine said.

"You didn't have anything to do with his death, did you Lorenzo?" said Vito.

"No, Godfather. I would have no reason to do such a thing," Constatine said. "And I would never do anything like that without your blessing."

"And Rocco? What about him?" Vito said.

"No, Godfather. Rocco would never do that," he said.

"Yes, I agree," Vito said. "Rocco is a little headstrong, young and ambitious, but he is a good soldier. Still, someone killed Dominic and the question is why?"

Chapter 54

Detective Martin placed a call to Attorney Carter Manning at his office.

"Mr. Manning, this is Detective Harvey Martin. Do you have a minute to talk?"

"Of course, Detective. I was going to call you. Are you calling about the reported death in the paper of Dominic Falucci?" Carter said.

"Yes," Martin said.

"I just read about it in the paper. What the hell?" said Carter.

"We really don't know, Martin replied. "It looks like a professional hit. No clues, no witnesses. I would like to talk with your client, Bob Conners. Do you have a telephone contact number for him? He should be advised of Falucci's death."

"What? Yes, of course. You don't think he had anything to do with this, do you?" said Carter.

"I don't know. Do you?" Martin replied.

"No. I know he was very bitter about what happened. I'm sure there will be no tears over Falucci when he hears the news, if he doesn't already know. I doubt that the report of his death would have been picked up in the Houston paper."

"I can't rule out any involvement. Not yet, anyway," said Martin. "That's the reason I need to contact him."

"I do have a number for him. He called to the office one time and we made a note of that. I am assuming he is still with the same company, but even if not, they could give you a forwarding address," said Carter.

"What is that number?" asked Martin.

Chapter 55

Bob Conners' secretary buzzed him in his office in Houston.

"Mr. Conners, there is a Detective Harvey Martin from Memphis asking to speak to you. Shall I put him through?"

"Yes, Patti, it's probably about Sally's death," said Bob.

"Hello, Detective. What can I do for you?" Bob said as he answered his phone.

"Mr. Conners, this is Detective Harvey Martin, in Memphis. We met once when your car was at the impound lot. Do you remember?"

"Yes, Detective. I remember quite well all the 'events' that befell my life and family in Memphis," he responded dryly. "Why are you calling?"

"We are doing an investigation on the death of Dominic Falucci. I believe he is the man who bought your house out of bankruptcy," said Martin.

"Falucci is dead?" asked Conners in a shocked voice.

"Yes, sir. He is. He was murdered two days ago. I have to ask you, sir, can you account for your whereabouts and activities two days ago?" asked Martin.

"Wait, wait, just a minute. Do you think I had something to do with his death?" demanded Conners.

"We want to rule out any number of things, Mr. Conners, and we need to know if you have an alibi for the time of his death," said Martin.

"What is the time frame?" asked Bob. "I have been here in Houston. I can't believe this!"

"It was a couple of days before his body was discovered," said Martin. The coroner has placed his time of death on Tuesday, sometime in the early afternoon, between 2:00 p.m. to 6:00 p.m."

"I had a business meeting out of town on Tuesday. I flew to Phoenix and was in a meeting during that time period. You can check and verify that with the company, Justin Oil, if you must. I can put my secretary on the line and she can give you the number for the company. I met with an Assistant Vice-President, Tom Walker, about an oil contract we are negotiating," said Bob.

"Yes, sir. I will hold on," replied Martin.

Chapter 56

After checking on Bob's alibi with Justin Oil Company, Detective Martin called Special Agent Simon to bring her up to speed on the Falucci investigation.

"Well, I appreciate your calling, Detective, but I don't have much connection with or interest in Falucci's death," she said.

"I know that. I'm hoping that we can have a mutual exchange of information," Martin said. "I checked on Conners and he has a very solid alibi for the Tuesday time that the coroner says was the window when Falucci was killed. He was in Phoenix in a meeting on Tuesday and his flight back to Houston didn't get in until 6:35 p.m., so I think he can be ruled out as a person of interest for the time being. This doesn't mean, however, that he couldn't have contracted with the killer."

"Do you think he seems like a person to do that? Where would he find a professional contract killer?" she asked.

"No, he doesn't, but I have learned to consider everything until I know otherwise," said Martin. "Who knows what a man will do to avenge the death of his wife? I don't, do you?"

"Until everything is ruled out, it's not ruled out," she agreed. "Now the only thing I can tell you is that we believe that we have located Lorenzo Constatine. He is in the New Jersey compound of Vito Carmine. Do you have enough to get a warrant?"

"Not even close," he replied, "but I would like to talk to him. We can put him in the car, if the finger print holds up. Not too good, really, and even if we did talk with him, he wouldn't say anything."

"I think the only thing I, or we, can do at this point is to follow up on the death of the Judge as not being a suicide," Martin said. I found a possible access to the terrace of the Judge's condo and a broken branch, so, theoretically, it is possible, or it was possible, for someone to climb up on the terrace."

Martin continued, "If the Judge didn't lock the sliding glass doors to the patio, and that is a possibility according to the cleaning lady, it would not be difficult to enter the condo, shoot the Judge with his own gun and leave the same way."

"As you know, there was gunshot residue on the Judge's right hand, but the Judge was left-handed. The killer wouldn't know that and might, or did, assume that he was right-handed and smeared gun residue on his right hand. That could be done with the gun in a plastic baggie. The killer takes the baggie, turns it inside out and smears it on the Judge's hand."

"If that happened, and I say, 'if,' a piece of the plastic might have entered with the bullet," she said.

"And, if so, all that proves is that he was murdered, which is what we think anyway. That doesn't get us the killer," he said. "Not worth another autopsy."

"And, if Falucci was responsible, or paid someone to kill him, Falucci is dead. No pun intended, we are at a dead end," said Agent Simon.

"Yeah," said Martin. "No footprints, no fingerprints, no forcible entry. That brings us back to square one," said Martin. "Falucci probably had Constatine kill Mrs. Conners to pull off the survivorship angle and to make some money through the sale of the house, but we can't prove it, then the Judge realizes what has happened and threatens to rat on Falucci, though he has no proof he can turn over to any law enforcement agency to connect him. Falucci doesn't like the idea that the Judge is going to give him grief, like he threatened to do, so he hires on a contract killer to kill the Judge. Problem solved."

"And," she said, "we are left with a question we can't answer. Who killed Falucci? And why?"

"Can I buy you a cup of coffee?" asked Martin.

"How about a drink?" she answered.

Chapter 57

Detective Harvey Martin and Special Agent Rachel Simon were sitting in a quiet and secluded booth at The Vault, a bar close to the Federal Building where she worked. They were both off duty so he had ordered a scotch and water and she had a gimlet, which they both nursed as they got to know each other a little better.

They both agreed that their first meeting at the Judge's condo was a little fractious, since she had pulled a gun on him and dropped into a shooter's stance. Martin didn't have much of an excuse as to why he was in the dead Judge's residence, but his credentials and a badge as a Detective for the Memphis Police Department got him a pass from being dropped on the floor and hand-cuffed. They both let that pass.

Martin said, "So what do we do now?"

Agent Simon said, "We have to wait for a break. Someone knows an awful lot about what happened."

"I don't think much of sitting around and waiting. What can we do to press the investigation? Like I said, when you can't find any clues, you're not looking hard enough," said Martin.

"Well," she said, "you said you found a possible entry to the Judge's condo by someone climbing up to the terrace. Did you canvass the area?"

"Um, not much to canvass. You can't get fingerprints off a tree branch and it was at night. I checked and there are no cameras on the Riverwalk Trail and none on the Judge's patio either. No footprints in the garden area and no fingerprints on the glass door from the patio to the living room area. Whoever did this was very careful. Professional I would say," said Martin.

"What about the gun?" she asked. "Where did that come from?"

"More than likely, it was the Judge's gun," replied Martin. "His daughter said that he had qualified on a shooting range, presumably with that gun. Maybe, maybe not. It was an older model Smith and Wesson police special, .38 caliber. She thinks her father might have inherited it from his father. He ran a dry goods store during the depression years and may have had it for his own protection of his store from robbery."

"Ballistics matched the bullet with the gun?" she asked.

"Yeah. The bullet that killed him came from that gun," he said.

"So how did the killer, if there was one, get the gun and shoot the judge in his bed with his own gun?" she asked. Presumably, he was asleep when he was shot based on the fact that he was still in bed. And there was no blood other than that on the bed. So the killer either had the gun or knew where it was in the Judge's residence, unless he brought it, which I suppose he could have. We can theorize it was the Judge's gun but we don't know if it was."

Martin thought about what she had just said.

"If the killer wanted to make it look like a suicide, which presumably he did, then you're right. He either brought a gun that can't be traced, or we are supposed to think it was the Judge's gun because he left it lying on the floor. If it was the Judge's gun, then the killer knew the Judge had one, found it and used it," said Martin.

"He or she wouldn't have gone to the residence by climbing up a tree hoping to find a gun," Rachel said.

"That leaves just those two possibilities. The killer either brought the gun or he used the Judge's gun, and if the killer knew the Judge had a gun, how did he or she know that, or more importantly, how did they know it was in his residence," he said.

She replied, "And also where he kept it?"

"Damn," Martin replied, "Occam's razor!"

"What?" she asked.

"Occam's razor. It's a theorem that says that of two explanations that account for the facts, the simpler one is more likely to be correct," said Martin.

"Okay," she said quizzically. "What is the answer?"

"The bug man," he said.

"What?" she asked.

Martin replied, "The cleaning lady said that she had let in a pest control man to service the Judge's residence a couple of days before his death."

"And?" she said.

"And she said that the Judge had a monthly contract with a pest control service to come spray to prevent ants and bugs that may come from his fruit trees," he said.

"And," Rachel said patiently.

"Yeah, and she said he was from the pest control company that the Judge regularly used," he said.

"So?" she asked.

"He wasn't the regular guy," he said, "and he had an opportunity to go into every room and closet."

"And found the gun!" she exclaimed.

"And found the gun," he said.

"Do you think he worked for the company?" she asked.

"No," he replied. "He is the killer. He used that cover to get into the Judge's residence to formulate his plan."

"Can the cleaning lady identify him?" she asked.

"She should be able to, she let him in the apartment," he said.

"Great!" she said. "Maybe we can get an artist's drawing and with any luck, he might be in a mug shot book. If so, we have an identity to pursue."

"Occam's razor," she said with a grin. "I didn't know you read philosophy."

"I think I read it in a comic strip," he said smiling at her.

Chapter 58

Martin had Maria meet with a police artist and she had a very good memory of the man in the pest control uniform. If he wasn't wearing a disguise, which was possible, then they had a pretty good likeness to compare photographs in the several mug shot books.

He was fairly certain that the man who he had decided was the Judge's killer did not work for the pest control company the Judge used, but he took the composite to the company personnel manager at Baker Pest Control to be sure.

"I don't recognize this man at all, officer," said the company's personnel manager as he looked at the drawing.

"It's Detective," Martin said. "I really didn't think this man worked for your company, but I needed to check it out. This man had a uniform with your company's logo on it. I don't know if he had a I.D. badge or not, but the cleaning lady who let him in thought it was a legitimate visit to spray the Judge's residence or, presumably, she would not have let him in. Let me ask, where do you get your uniforms for your service people."

"They are ordered locally from Uniform Supply here in Memphis," the Manager said. "I guess anyone could go there and ask for a new uniform. They also make the logo patch on the uniform. They wouldn't have an identification badge, however, and we do require all of our service persons to have a photo I.D. badge. They also aren't supposed to go inside unless it is a specific request or the contract calls for it. If they do, then they wear baggies over their shoes. Don't want to track anything in, you know. Residents don't like that."

"Was there a request by the Judge for a service call?" asked Martin.

"What day was this man there?" asked the manager. "I will check and see.

"It would have been last Tuesday," said Martin.

"No," replied the manager. "I don't see any special request for a service call for that date. The Judge's condo has a regular monthly contract and we service his place on the first Tuesday of the month, so it has already been treated this month as usual."

"Have any of your employees reported any uniform or I.D. badge missing?" asked Martin.

"No, not to my knowledge, but an I.D. badge wouldn't do anyone any good, unless they changed the photo, which I guess someone could, I mean paste a photo over a duplicate or something like that," replied the manager.

"Yeah, something like that," said Martin.

"But, Detective, we aren't armed guards at a bank. We run a pest control company. We've never had an imposter use our uniform or I.D. badge to go into someone's home without the owner's authorization," he said.

"Until now," he replied.

Chapter 59

Martin's next stop was the Memphis Uniform Supply Company that made up the uniforms for Baker Pest Control. After greeting the Manager of that company and telling him what he was investigating, he asked if there had been a recent request for a new uniform.

"Let me see, Detective, yes, we did make up a new uniform for an employee about 10 days ago. Nothing unusual there as we have requests all the time for new uniforms. The pest control service people have to go under houses all the time and they get their uniforms soiled on a regular basis. The company doesn't want their service people going around in soiled uniforms so I thought nothing about it. We send a bill to Baker each month if we have made up a new uniform. Haven't billed them yet for this month, however," said the manager.

"Might the clerk who took the order be here?" Martin asked.

"Yes, I believe she is. Let me call her from the front counter," he said.

The young lady named Missy who responded to the Manager's call came and looked at the composite photo.

"Yes," she said. "I recognize that person. I remember him because he was thin and looked very athletic, and he was good looking," she said sheepishly. I took his measurements for the uniform as he said he was a new employee. We have most, if not all, of the Baker service people on file for their uniform size. That's a pretty good likeness. He picked up the uniform, oh, let's see, last Thursday, I think. He offered to pay for it, but I said we would bill the company."

"What name did he give you as an employee?" Martin asked. "Let's see, I'm sure I wrote it on the ticket. Have to in order to bill the company. Here it is: James Foster."

Martin didn't even have to call Baker Pest Control. He knew there was no James Foster as an employee. He did call nevertheless because he was thorough. No James Foster. *What a surprise,* he thought to himself.

"Do you have his measurements on file?" Martin asked.

"Oh yes," replied the manager. "I will make you a copy."

One more piece to the puzzle, thought Martin, and since Missy the clerk recognized him from the composite drawing that Marie had provided, it meant that he wasn't wearing a disguise when he entered the Judge's residence. Got lucky on that. They always make a mistake.

Time to hit the mug books.

Chapter 60

"His name is Rocco Solvano," Rachel said, "and he has a record, obviously, or he wouldn't be in our data base. Petty theft and carjacking, nothing big time. He was sentenced to 11/29 for taking a stolen car across state lines, which made it a federal crime, released after six months for good behavior. He completed his parole and disappeared according to his parole officer."

"Well, he's in the big time now," replied Martin. "No way of knowing where he is now?"

"No. No wants or warrants on him at present," she said.

"I want him," Martin replied. "Come on, you're the feds, the F.B.I., you know everything about everybody and you can't tell me where you think he might be?"

"Contrary to popular opinion, Detective, we don't have a satellite laser tracking everyone's movements," she replied indignantly.

"Okay. Don't get all wadded up," he said.

"I'm not," she replied.

"Is there any chance that he might have hooked up with the Carmine family? I mean, Constatine is there and we are pretty sure that he came down to Memphis to do the Conners woman, and we know there were two of them because they had two cars. What are the chances young Rocco came down with Big Connie for a car heist and it turned into a lot more than that?" he asked.

"Maybe Rocco has graduated to big time. What if Dominic thought a lot of him and gave him an opportunity to 'make his bones' as they say."

"Knocking off a federal judge? Some bones," she said.

"Hey, it's the mafia, not the Boy Scouts," he replied. "You don't get to be a capo without showing some moxie."

"I'll see what I can find out from the New Jersey office," she replied. "Maybe someone has seen him around the Carmine compound."

"That a girl. Now you're talking," he said.

Chapter 61

Rachel called Harvey and told him that the F.B.I. office in Trenton, New Jersey, had spotted Rocco Solvano. Trenton was the home place of the Carmine family.

"Can you pick him up?" asked Martin.

"On what charge?" she replied.

"Suspicion," he said.

"Oh, really. Suspicion of what," she answered.

"I don't know. The F.B.I. can always think of something, can't they?" he said.

"There you go again," she replied haughtily. "No. We can't just pick up someone on 'suspicion.' Besides, if we did, the Carmine attorneys would have him out of jail before we turned the key. Don't be stupid."

"I'm not. I'm just trying to solve two murders," he said.

"Shall we meet at The Vault. That always seems to be a good source of our combined brain power," he said.

"Sure, why not. I will see you there about 5 o'clock," she replied.

When they met in their designated booth and had ordered their "usuals," Martin said, "We need to analyze what we have and see where it takes us."

"Okay," she replied as she sipped her gimlet.

He began, "We know, or think we know, that Falucci hired Constatine to come down to Memphis and run the Conners woman off the road. We know that this was part of Falucci's scheme to make quick money off the purchase of this survivorship interest from the bankruptcy trustee for little money and then selling the property for a big profit."

"Okay, no proof of any of this, but continue," she replied.

"And we know that Constatine brought young Rocco with him to Memphis because he knew he would need another driver and Rocco knew how to steal a car. Let's assume that Falucci knew Constatine, but never met up with Rocco."

"Okay, so far," she said.

Martin continued, "Okay, so Big Connie and Rocco steal the Mercedes and watch and wait for the opportune time when they can force Mrs. Conners' car off the embankment and down into Nonconnah Creek, where she drowns in her car. Nothing to indicate it is anything other than an accident, right?"

"Yes, except for the damage to the Mercedes, which matched up with the damage to the Conners' car and shows that the Mercedes was the car that hit, or pushed, the Conners' car down the embankment," she said.

"Right," he said and continued, "and Connie and Rocco then take the car down in the hood where they expect it is going to be stolen and whoever is caught with the car, they're going to take the fall. The witness, Tyrone, would be able to identify the man who we think is Constatine, when he got out of the Mercedes."

"Okay, so far," she replied.

"But Connie has left some cigarette butts in the Mercedes, so we can, maybe, put him as the driver when the Conners' car got pushed down the embankment. Only way to prove that is if Rocco testifies to that, which is not likely. Now so far everything is going exactly as Falucci planned. He has bought the survivorship interest from the trustee in bankruptcy, bumped off the surviving widow and then had the right to sell the Conners' house, which he did."

"Now the plan has gone just like Falucci thought it would, and he has made a quarter of a million dollars after the sale of the house. No entanglements, everything was legal."

"Except for murdering a housewife with two children and a husband," said Rachel.

"Yeah, but that doesn't bother him. It does bother the bankruptcy judge, however, when he realizes what has happened and what Falucci has done, and the Judge feels that he may be responsible in some way. The Judge is very upset, but he knows that what Falucci did is legal and that he has no proof whatsoever that Falucci is responsible for the Conners' woman's death."

"So the Judge confronts Falucci, who he knows from wherever in his background, and says he is going to try and make sure that Falucci is somehow found guilty of murdering the Conners woman."

"Falucci starts to get a little hot under the collar about what the Judge knows or thinks he knows," says Rachel.

"Right, and Falucci threatens the Judge to make him back off, which scares the Judge. After all, he thinks that Falucci has already killed or had the Conners woman killed in furtherance of his scheme.

"So the Judge writes this 'in case of my death letter' so Falucci won't skate," she says.

"Bingo, but Falucci doesn't know about the letter. He decides anyway that he can't take the chance that the Judge is not going to rat on him in some way and decides that the Judge has to be taken out of the picture."

Rachel says, "Let me guess. He hires Rocco Solvano, a/k/a James Foster, to figure out a way to eliminate the Judge, and Rocco, being an enterprising young mafia hit man, suggests that the Judge's death needs to look like a suicide."

"You got it, you smart girl," says Martin. "Now Rocco comes and cases the Judge's condo as the bug man, and, lo and behold, he finds a gun that the Judge has in his condo when he 'sprays' all the areas in the house. This gives him the weapon with which to set up the Judge's 'suicide'."

"And," she says, "don't stop now."

"And," he continues, "Rocco being young and athletic sees while he is in the Judge's condo, that he can access the terrace from the Riverwalk by climbing up the slope with the help of the trees."

"And does so," she says.

"Yeah, and having already found the Judge's gun, and maybe even taken it when he was there previously, thinking the Judge doesn't check every night to see if his gun is where he left it, climbs the slope, gets on the terrace wearing booties to cover any footprints, opens the sliding glass doors, goes into the Judge's bedroom, who is sound asleep, and pops him with his own gun. Presto, it's a suicide," Martin said. "He may even have used a baggie over his hand to collect the gun shot residue, which he then rubs on the Judge's right hand."

"But," she says excitedly, "he doesn't know the Judge is left-handed, and rubs the GSR on his right hand!"

"Exactly," said Martin, "but it will never hold up in court that a left-handed man can't use his right hand to shoot himself in the right temple. So, anyway, Rocco leaves the gun on the floor by the bed where he thinks it would have fallen had the Judge shot himself."

"Okay, assuming I buy all of that, which is a lot of supposition," she said, "who killed Falucci? And why?"

"Now that is the question, isn't it," he replied. "Let's look at the possible persons of interest: Vito Carmine, who is totally pissed off at his nephew, Dominic, who he thinks is a moron and who may have killed a Federal Judge. This is going to bring down all kinds of heat on him and his family, and he decides that Dominic has made too many mistakes; or we have the Judge's daughter, whom we know nothing about, but she has the letter from her father and as far as she knows, Falucci is going to skate, since her father's death has been ruled a suicide, if he killed her father; or we have the Judge's loyal secretary of many years, also of whom we know nothing about, i.e. either one may have connections we don't know of; or, we have the Conners' woman's husband who could certainly want his pound of flesh and avenge his wife's death, whether he can trace that death to Falucci or not, he knows that Falucci is Worthmore Financial and his greed lost him his wife, his house and his previously pleasant life, notwithstanding he himself has an alibi for the time of Falucci's death; or again relying on

Occam's razor, we have the dark horse, Rocco Solvano. My money is on him."

"But why would Rocco want to kill Falucci?" she asked.

"Because," Martin continued. "If Falucci hired him to hit the Judge, from that point on, Falucci owned him. Solvano had already killed once. What was to keep him from eliminating Falucci and continuing his career as a hit man. He can't go to the electric chair twice and in killing Falucci, if he did, he was practicing his new trade craft. Only flaw there is placating the Godfather if Vito didn't want Dominic out of his hair and he finds out that Rocco was the hit man. And, finally, we have any number of unknown enemies Falucci has collected over a period of time as a result of his schemes or crimes. Someone who has no connection with this case, but wanted him dead."

"If," she said. "Can you prove any of this?" she asked.

"No," came the reply. "I can't. Not yet anyway."

"And maybe never," she said.

"Yeah, that too," he said. "But I'll keep trying. Something will break."

Chapter 62

After they left The Vault, Harvey continued to think about what he and Rachel had pieced together about what they knew and what they didn't. While the death of the judge was being classified as a suicide as far as the MPD and the FBI were concerned, he just couldn't seem to accept that conclusion. He knew, as Rachel had said, that there was a lot of supposition to his theory. He didn't really have any "facts" per se. He went back to his condo and decided he would make up his own murder book.

When he actually had what homicide detectives called a "murder book," it contained all the information about suspects, photographs, interviews and whatever it had or might have in connection to an actual murder. He often found that when he went over the content of the murder book, he would find something that was missing that often gave him a clue which might eventually lead to a solution.

He decided that if he could prove that the judge was, in fact, murdered, he could work his way back to suspects and that might lead to solving Falucci's murder as well. He was confident that all of these events were connected.

He began by looking at the photographs of the judge's body. The photographs taken by the coroner showed the body in a fully reclined position as a person asleep on his left side. He thought that if a person were in bed, under covers with a conscious intention to shoot himself, he would be sitting up, perhaps, and not lying down.

The judge's body was not on its back, so there was a strong presumption in his mind that the judge had been asleep when he was shot by his murderer. The photographs showed a single bullet wound to the right temple, which would indicate a difficult posture for one to shoot oneself, and even more so for a left-handed person. It was as if someone stood over the body and shot downward into the judge's right temple and left the body otherwise undisturbed.

And there is the position of the gun on the floor. Yes, it was likely that if a person shot himself, the recoil of the gun would cause the gun to fall to the floor, so the position of the gun was not remarkable.

What was remarkable was the GSR on the judge's right hand as determined by the coroner's examination. The dusting of the hand indicated a swabbing effect on the top of the hand, but no splatter effect as might be expected, and even more remarkable, there was no GSR on the bed covers. None.

These were facts. Facts that convinced Martin that the shooter had put a baggie of some kind over his hand before firing the gun, capturing the GSR that would have been expelled by the bullet. The shooter must have then turned the baggie inside out and swabbed the judge's right hand with the gun shot residue and placed the gun on the floor by the bedside. That explained why there was no residue on the bed covers or any other proximity.

Martin called Patsy Chalmers.

"Miss Chalmers, this is Detective Harvey Martin. I know it's late and I hope I'm not disturbing you, but I am going to need your approval for something," Martin said.

"Of course, Detective," she replied, "and it's not too late. I am up reading. What do you need?"

"I would like you to give permission for your father's body to be exhumed. I think, if I find what I believe I will find upon further examination, that I can prove that your father was murdered and did not commit suicide," Martin said.

"I don't know," she said. "What do you think you will find if you do exhume his body?"

"If I'm right, I expect that an examination of the bullet wound will expose a tiny bit of plastic from a plastic bag. I believe that the person who shot your father put a plastic bag over his hand that held the gun before he fired it," he said.

"You think someone shot my father and that he didn't commit suicide?" she asked.

"Yes," replied Martin.

"Does this have something to do with his fear for his life as he wrote in the letter?" she asked.

"Yes," Martin replied. "I think his fear was justified. If that tiny bit of plastic can be recovered, if it is there, then we can be certain that your father was murdered, and I think I know how it was done."

Chapter 63

Martin knew that since Judge Chalmers' death had been ruled a suicide that it was unlikely an autopsy had been performed and he was right. It had not, and asking the judge's daughter to give permission to exhume the body was one thing. Asking her to give permission to perform an autopsy, limited as it would be, was quite another. He was, therefore, surprised to get a call from Patsy Chalmers.

"Detective Martin, this is Patsy Chalmers. I have been thinking about what you asked and if it will, in your opinion, prove that my father was murdered, then I will give permission to exhume his body. What do you think an examination will show?" she said.

"Miss Chalmers, I want to be completely honest with you. The bullet will have to be removed from your father's brain and that will require some desecration of his skull. As to what I expect from this examination, I can only hypothesize for you, but I expect that a small fragment of a plastic baggie may have been encased with the bullet. I cannot give you absolute assurance of this. I wish I could," said Martin.

"How would that have happened, I mean, how would the fragment of plastic get embedded in the wound, if I understand what you are saying?" she said.

"I believe that the killer of your father put the pistol in a plastic baggie before pulling the trigger. The purpose of doing this was to capture the gun shot residue, which we call the GSR. He, or she, wanted to do this in order to smear the GSR on your father's hand in order to make it look like your father had used the gun on himself, hence the suicide argument. The flaw in trying to show it was suicide and not murder was that the GSR was rubbed on his right hand, not his left, and as you know, your father was left-handed," said Martin.

"Yes," replied Patsy, "he was left-handed, but that doesn't mean he couldn't have used his right hand to pull the trigger, if he did, in fact, commit suicide."

"I realize that," Martin said, and that is why I can't say for certain that he was murdered. The other detectives think it was a clear case of suicide. I want you to know that so you can make a fully informed decision before you agree to exhume the body and that you understand that the examination might not show what we believe, or rather, what I believe."

"What happens if what you believe turns out to be true, that is, that my father was murdered?" asked Patsy. "What happens next?"

"We do our dead level best to find out who killed him and why. Why is the big question, and I think I know why?" said Martin.

"Why?" she asked.

"The judge spelled it out in his letter that he left for you. He knew too much about Falucci and threatened to try to convince the attorney general that Mrs. Conners was murdered. Falucci couldn't have that hanging over his head, even though there was little or no evidence that connected him to her death," said Martin.

"And Mrs. Conners' death was necessary for Falucci to get the Conners' house?" she asked.

"Yes," he said, "and your father was very bothered about what he believed to be true. It wasn't enough for him to commit suicide, but it certainly bothered him," said Martin, "or he wouldn't have written that letter. He was consciously aware of the fact that his own life might be in danger. If Falucci killed once, or had Mrs. Conners killed, he wouldn't hesitate to do so again."

"I think," said Patsy, "that we have to know what happened. I will give my consent to the exhumation."

"And the examination?" Martin asked.

"Yes," she said, "and the examination."

Chapter 64

"And she has agreed to that?" said Rachel.

"Yes, and she has to sign a permission order to exhume the body," said Martin. "We can only hope that the evidence that we think is there will be there."

"And if it isn't?" she asked.

"Then we look for something else to prove the judge was murdered," he said.

"That will be difficult," she said.

"But not impossible. Someone shot him. We have got to prove that with or without physical evidence," he said.

"That means we have to find that person and prove that he, or she, did it."

"She?" she asked.

"No one is ruled out, until they are ruled out," he said, "but I agree the chances of a woman being somehow involved are slim and none.

The man who posed as the bug technician in order to get into the judge's condo in all likelihood did it as a lone wolf, likely hired. As I said, my bet is on Rocco having been hired by Falucci."

"And then Rocco killed the golden goose that would keep him in his chosen profession?" she asked.

"Why would he do that other than as you say 'Falucci then owns him?'"

"That I don't know. It's possible that Rocco didn't know his contract was on a Federal judge," said Martin, "and maybe that spooked him. Who knows what goes on in the mind of a hired killer?"

"Even if the judge's death was ruled a suicide?" she asked.

"It was a 'perfect crime.' Falucci should have been pleased with the result. As I would think Rocco was."

"Yeah, I agree that it is a stretch to put Falucci's death on Rocco," said Martin, "but the suspects would have to be limited, perhaps to someone that really had a grudge against him and wanted to see him dead."

"And," she replied, "that could be a number of people. We don't know that much about Falucci. He might have swindled a bunch of people. This buying a 'right of survivorship' and then killing off the surviving spouse indicates an inventive mind."

"That's certainly a possibility," he said, "but Falucci didn't have a criminal record."

"Which brings us back to your 'Occam's Razor,' doesn't it?" she said, grinning at Martin.

"Meaning?" he asked.

"Who are the most logical suspects?" she asked. "Those currently on the radar who would want to see Falucci get his just desserts as a matter of retribution. An eye for an eye."

"Hmmm," Martin mused.

Chapter 65

With Patsy Chalmers, the judge's only surviving heir, having given permission and authorization to exhume her father's body, the police coroner began his grisly job of digging into the skull to remove the bullet. Martin had told him what he was looking for, so the exploration of the cavity had to be deftly performed. There had been no autopsy as such since the death had been ruled a suicide and the wound was intact as the doctor probed delicately.

Retrieving the bullet was not difficult, but looking for a tiny piece of plastic, if it existed, was, and if it were to be found, it would mean the judge had, in fact, been murdered as Martin thought he had.

The coroner placed a call to Harvey Martin.

"Detective Martin?" he asked when the phone was answered. "This is Coroner Ralph Bates. You asked me to call you after I had done the exploratory of the skull and brain tissue of the judge's gunshot wound."

"Yes, Dr. Bates," said Martin with great anxiety. "What did you find?"

"I have recovered a .38 caliber bullet from the cavity and it is intact," said the coroner.

"And, anything else?" Martin said impatiently.

"Yes," said the doctor, "it does appear that there is the tiniest piece of what appears to be non-tissue that was located ahead of the trajectory of the bullet, or rather buried by the bullet. That's what you thought I might find, correct?"

"Yes," said Martin excitedly. "Exactly. That little bit of non-tissue, as you have described it, could it be plastic? That would indicate that the shooter had, perhaps, wrapped his hand in a plastic baggie of some kind before pulling the trigger. Can you think of any reason why someone who wanted to commit suicide by shooting themselves in the temple would put their hand in a plastic bag before doing that, doctor?"

"No, Detective, that would be a strange thing to do," said Coroner Bates. "It is not something that I have experienced in my practice or in my years of examining suicides or in examining gunshot wounds. Certainly I have found cloth or pieces of detritus carried into the cavity by a bullet, but not a piece of what appears to me to be part of a plastic bag in what is purported to be a suicide."

"And, if the person did that, doctor, is there any way that the baggie would not still be with the body?" asked Martin.

"Only if someone removed it from his hand after the shot," said the doctor. "Was a baggie found at the scene?"

"No, doctor, no baggie was found on his hand or on the bed. Only the gun on the floor," said Martin.

"Then in my opinion, the supposition that this man committed suicide is called into question," said Dr. Bates.

"Indeed it is, doctor, indeed it is," replied Martin.

Chapter 66

Harvey Martin called Rachel when he got the opinion of the coroner that called the ruling of suicide into question.

"Really?" she said, when he told her that the doctor had found a piece of what he had described as 'non-tissue' in the wound, presumably a plastic fragment, most likely from a baggie.

"Really," he said. "And the fact that no baggie was found at the scene, in my opinion, means we have a crime and not a suicide."

"Have you spoken to the judge's daughter and told her?"

"No, not yet," he replied. "I will. I thought this result might want the FBI to take another look at what now is logically a crime scene and a crime."

"Yes, we will," she replied. "Is the doctor writing his findings in a report?"

"Yes, and he has preserved the non-tissue item and it is available to give to you for further examination and identification. The FBI lab should be able to do that, right?" he said.

"Yes, Harvey," she sniffed, "the FBI can do that."

"And, of course," he added, "there was no baggie found at the scene, which could only mean that the killer took it with him. Perhaps the FBI can find out how he gained entry and how he left without being seen."

"You think he climbed up to the terrace, right?"

"I'm actually pretty certain of it," he replied. "I can see a broken branch in the tree just below the judge's overlook. If he gained entrance that way, he more than likely left the condo the same way. No one was there on the River Walk Trail to see his coming and going. That no one heard the shot is a bit of a mystery, but perhaps the baggie or whatever he used to capture the GSR muffled the noise of the gun."

"Perhaps," she said. "So what happens now, besides your turning over the specimen to the FBI, which you will do, right?"

"Of course," he replied. "As to what happens now may depend on what the FBI discovers at the condo. Clearly this is not going to be enough to open a murder book at the MPD."

"At least not yet," she replied.

Chapter 67

Martin called Patsy Chalmers as he said he would to inform her of the coroner's finding what he thought might be found on examination.

"Miss Chalmers?" he asked as the phone was answered. "This is Detective Martin. We have completed, or rather the coroner has completed, a further examination of the bullet wound."

"Yes, Detective, I've been waiting to hear from you or from someone," she said. "Did you find what you were looking for?"

"Yes, Ma'am," he replied. "The coroner did find a tiny fragment of non-tissue which we believe is part of a plastic sack or baggie of some kind. That has been turned over to the FBI for further analysis, and they will now carefully inspect your father's condo, which was not done by the MPD since the ruling was that his death was a suicide."

"And you think that this man, Falucci, was responsible for his death?" she asked.

"I do," he replied.

"And he was murdered, is that right?" she asked.

"Yes, without a doubt about that," he replied.

"Who do you think might have done that?" she asked.

"Right now, that is an unknown. We have no suspects and little evidence, other than recovering the bullet from the autopsy," he said. "Obviously, there was a person, or people, who wanted to see him dead. Why is the question, but revenge of some type has to be on the top of the list."

Chapter 68

As he promised to do, Martin retrieved the non-tissue item that the coroner had preserved in a test tube and turned it over to Rachel, who dutifully took it to the FBI crime lab for identification and analysis. She also let the Special Agent in Charge know what the current status of Martin's investigation had revealed about the judge's death.

"So," said the SAC, "Martin has convinced himself that Judge Chalmers was murdered."

"Yes, he has," she replied, "and he presents a pretty good case. We need to follow up on what he has uncovered, starting with what the crime lab can tell us about the piece of non-tissue that is being examined. It certainly appears to the human eye that it is foreign matter of some kind, not human tissue, and more than likely plastic of some kind. Since it was found in the bullet hole, ahead of the bullet, the only way it could have gotten there is for the bullet to have forced it ahead of the trajectory."

"What do you think it is? asked the SAC."

"Personally, I don't know, but Martin thinks it is a piece of a plastic bag of some kind," she replied.

"So, if the judge was shot," he continued, "the weapon was within a plastic bag of some kind?"

"Yes," she said, "that way the GSR could be preserved and rubbed on the judge's hand to make it appear further that he shot himself."

"What did the investigation indicate about the GSR?" he asked.

"It was found on the judge's right hand, but it appeared to be swabbed and was just on the top of his hand. The MPD lab didn't find any evidence of gunshot residue on his fingers, and the amount on the top of his hand was not in a spray pattern like you would expect," she said.

"Was it the judge's gun?" he asked.

"There's no way of knowing that," she replied. "The gun was an older revolver, a .38 caliber Smith & Wesson and it can't be traced because of its age, probably manufactured and sold in the 1920s. His daughter never knew he had a gun."

"Anything else?" he asked.

"Yes," she said. "The judge was shot in the right temple and his body was positioned as if he were asleep on his side and the killer stood over him when he pulled the trigger."

"He wasn't sitting up in the bed?" he asked.

"No," she replied. "Not a normal position for someone who was going to shoot himself. And, there is one other thing."

"What's that?" the SAC asked.

"The judge was left-handed," she said.

"So?"

"It would be unusual for a left-handed person to shoot himself in the right temple," she said, "even though it is physically possible."

"Yes," he replied, "I see what you mean about questions on it being ruled a suicide. What about entry into the judge's residence? Any evidence of forcible entry?"

"No," she said. "But according to Martin, there is a way to reach the overlook at the judge's condo, and he is pretty certain that the investigating detectives didn't bother to follow up on anything once they had decided it was a suicide."

"What makes him think the killer might have, what, climbed up to the overlook and gotten in that way?" he asked.

"He says that the overlook can be reached from below by using the River Walk Trail and climbing up a tree that might provide access. He says he found a broken branch high up using binoculars. As far as we know, there were no footprints on the terrace, but it is likely no one looked very hard," she said.

"Any footprints found on the inside?" he asked.

"No, not that he knows of. The carpet is a short hard pile and it more than likely wouldn't show any. There was no evidence of mud or debris of any kind. Martin thinks that the killer probably wore booties over his shoes. He thinks that the killer might have gone into the judge's condo beforehand disguised as a pest control technician," she replied, "and the judge's cleaning lady was able to describe the man for an artist's drawing."

"Any I.D. from the drawing?" he asked.

"We think so. There is a small-time car thief named Rocco Solvano. He was in the mug books and the cleaning lady identified him as the pest control technician that came to the judge's condo to treat the residence for bugs, and an employee at the uniform company that the pest control company uses to provide uniforms for their employees also identified him as having come into the office to get a new uniform. He said he was a new employee. The company manager said he didn't work for them when shown the picture.

"Sounds like Martin has done a good bit of investigating in the case. Did he do this on his own?" he asked.

"Yes," she replied. "He simply doesn't believe it was a suicide, and he has to convince the MPD or us. The judge was a federal Bankruptcy Judge. Do we investigate it as a murder?"

"Let's see what the crime lab says about the foreign non-tissue item," the SAC said. "If it turns out to be a piece of plastic, we can look into it further. Why does Martin think it is part of a bag of some kind?"

"Two reasons," she replied. "One, it was for capturing the GSR, and two, it also probably muffled the gun shot, to some degree anyway. None of the neighbors said they heard anything that sounded like a gun shot."

"What do we have on Rocco?" he asked. "It's a big jump from being a car thief to a murderer of a federal judge."

"That's for sure," she replied. "We think he has become linked up with the Carmine family and is in New Jersey where the family is located.

"Interesting," he said. "Has he been located in New Jersey?"

"Yes," she said. "He has been seen by agents in Trenton where the family is based."

"How did he get down to Memphis?" he asked.

"Martin thinks that he and another man named Constatine were hired to come to Memphis by Anthony Falucci to kill a woman named Sally Conners. He is pretty certain that this was a scheme cooked up by Falucci to take the Conners' house after the husband filed a bankruptcy," she related. "It has to do with something called a 'right of survivorship,' which can be bought from the Bankruptcy Trustee. The survivor of a husband and wife's interest in jointly owned property gets the property when one of them dies. It's a little complicated when you have an intervening bankruptcy and only one of the married couples files a petition, but suffice it to say that the interest owned by the filing spouse can be bought. If the other spouse dies, the property goes to whoever bought the Trustee's interest. It's basically a gamble as to who might die first, unless you lower the odds by killing the surviving spouse."

"And that happened?" he asked.

"Yes, Martin believes it did, and Constatine and Rocco made sure by killing the wife," she said.

"And Falucci bought this survivorship interest?" he asked.

"Yes," she replied.

"Where is this Falucci now?" he asked.

"He's dead. Someone killed him," she replied.

"Wow," he said, "and all of this is related to the judge's death?"

"Yes. The judge knew Falucci and he wrote a letter to his daughter in which he stated that he feared for his life because he knew what Falucci did," she replied. "Evidently, his fears were justified."

"That is a tangled web," he said.

"When first we try to deceive," she replied.

"Keep me informed," he said.

"Will do," was her reply.

Chapter 69

Martin reviewed his self-prepared murder book as he often did when searching for something that he had either overlooked or not considered when analyzing a crime. In doing so, he kept coming up with the same persons whom he considered to be "interested" in what had developed.

He realized that he really didn't know much about any of them. What about the judge's secretary, or his daughter for that matter? Could they have had any involvement in Falucci's death? They certainly might have reason to, but how would that have come about, he asked himself? Could they have perhaps gotten together for some type of revenge?

He decided he needed to look into their backgrounds, but how to do this? Once again, he decided to call on Rachel to see if she could help.

"Rachel," said Martin as she answered his telephone call. "This is Harvey. Have you got a minute?"

She noticed that he was no longer "Detective Martin" and she was no longer "Agent Simon." She wondered if this new familiarity meant that their relationship had moved to another level. *If so,* she thought, *that might not be a bad thing.* She found Martin attractive and easy enough to talk to, but they had just talked about the developments or non-developments of the case. *Did she want to take it to a higher level,* she thought? *Did he?*

Rachel replied back to Martin in the affirmative. "Sure, Harvey, what is on your mind now?"

"Well," he said, "this may be more relevant to Falucci's murder than the judge's, but I'm trying to tie things together."

He continued, "I realized that we don't know anything about the judge's daughter or his secretary, for that matter. Can you do some background inquiry for me without involving the Bureau to any great extent?"

"Perhaps," she said. "The secretary is a federal employee, so her background before she was hired would be on her résumé, and as long as she didn't conceal anything, and that's not likely, hers would be readily available. The daughter is or may be another matter entirely. What do you think this might reveal, and more importantly, why are you interested in getting this information? As you say, Falucci's murder doesn't really have anything to do with who killed the judge, does it?"

"True, to some extent, unless whoever killed the judge also killed Falucci, but what if Falucci was killed by someone else for an entirely unrelated reason?" he said.

"Like?" she asked.

"Revenge for the judge's death or for the death of Sally` Conners, for that matter," he said.

"Oh, so now we have conspirators," she mused.

"Wouldn't be the first time," he replied.

"If it involves the Conners woman's death, wouldn't that involve her husband?" she asked.

"Possibly," was his response.

"I thought you had determined that he had a rock-solid alibi for the time of Falucci's death?" she said.

"Yeah, for him personally, but that doesn't mean he might not have had a role in it," said Martin.

"Harvey," she said laughingly, "have you been smoking something?"

"Okay, I admit this may be a little far-fetched," he said, "but I just want to know more about the background of those people who weren't torn up about Falucci's death.

"Well," she said, "that could include Uncle Vito as well, couldn't it."

"Yeah, I guess," he replied.

"Okay, I will see what I can find out quietly," she said.

Chapter 70

Rachel Simon began her task of researching the backgrounds of the three most likely persons that she and Martin had talked about, namely, Patsy Chalmers, the daughter, Bob Conners, the widower of Sally Conners, his wife, and the judge's secretary, Margaret Patterson, with little enthusiasm for Martin's conspiracy theory. She found nothing really remarkable about either the daughter or the husband.

Patsy Chalmers was a legal secretary in a big law firm in New York. She had grown up in Memphis, had gone to Hutchison School for Girls, a private school, and then on to Vanderbilt University in Nashville, Tennessee. She moved shortly after graduation and while interested in pursuing a legal career after her father's chosen profession, decided to get some experience before deciding whether she wanted to go to law school. She decided to become a legal secretary and was so employed when she got the news about her father.

Rachel saw nothing in her background that would in any way put her in the cross-hairs of the investigation. The only possible reason that the daughter might have in having any satisfaction in Falucci's death was, as Martin indicated, desire for revenge. But Patsy Chalmers just didn't seem to fit the type, and, of course, she hadn't even known that her father had been murdered, if he was, until after Martin followed up on the autopsy, and by that time, Falucci was already dead.

After eliminating the daughter from any conspiracy conjured up by Martin, she turned her attention to the next most likely person, the husband, Bob Conners.

Although Conners had served in the military in Vietnam and thus had some experience with weapons and combat, he also didn't seem to her that he might get involved, even though he did know, or could have known, that Falucci might have been involved in some way with his wife's death. But, she thought, if his involvement were to be discovered and he was criminally prosecuted, he would have left his two children in the lurch of foster care. Not a likely prospect, especially since he had moved to Houston, obtained a new executive position in his chosen field of expertise, and had put this sorrowful chapter in his life behind him.

Clearly, she thought, he would shed no tears at the news of Falucci's death, the man who took over his house and possibly ruined his life forever, but Martin had checked on his alibi and said it was good for the time of the death. Even if he could have now afforded to put some money in a plot to kill Falucci, there was nothing to indicate that he would know how to orchestrate such a hired killing. You can't just advertise in the paper for a murderer for hire. She discounted him as a likely suspect.

So that leaves Uncle Vito and the judge's secretary as two other considerations. While Vito Carmine could certainly put out a contract on his nephew, the big question would be why would he do such a thing.

Even if he were greatly upset with his nephew's get-rich-quick schemes, Dominic wouldn't have deserved being rubbed out. No, Uncle Vito was not a likely suspect either.

Rachel then turned her attention to Margaret Patterson, the judge's long-time secretary. In doing so, Rachel's eyebrows were raised when she found out that while Ms. Patterson had been the judge's secretary for twenty years, prior to that she had been an employee of the CIA.

"Well, I'll be damned," she said to herself when she read the federal investigative report prepared years earlier when she applied for the secretarial position. But that's all the report said, "previously an employee of the Central Intelligence Agency."

Rachel knew that getting further information from the CIA on a former employee and what she did there, was a total dead end. She was frankly surprised that this employment was even mentioned in her application, but there were a lot of people employed in perfectly ordinary capacities in the CIA. She could have been a secretary there as well and probably was, she thought. And then again, maybe not.

How, she thought, could she find out what Margaret Patterson, if that was her name, did while at the CIA? Was the job as the judge's secretary a cover in some way for former activities of a clandestine nature? Her imagination was going wild and she was very close to the judge.

"Oh, really, Rachel," she mused. "You are getting as bad as Harvey." But she wondered.

Chapter 71

"Harvey," said Rachel, "let's meet at the Vault this evening at 5. I have something very interesting to tell you."

"What is it?" he said quizzically.

"No, I will tell you then," she said.

Harvey Martin was waiting in their favorite booth when he saw Rachel come in. He had ordered her favorite drink, the Gimlet, and was sipping his scotch with great anticipation. She slid into the booth opposite him and looked like the cat who ate the canary.

"Okay, tell me," he said.

"You asked me to do backgrounds on our 'usual suspects' and so I did," she said. "I checked out four: The daughter, the husband, the secretary and Uncle Vito.

"And," he said.

"And, I have crossed off three of them as unlikely to have anything to do with Falucci's murder," she said.

"You mentioned four," he said. "One remaining that we should be interested in?"

"Yes," she said coyly. "Care to guess which one?"

Martin looked at her and thought about the four suspects that they had talked about. He had also done an elimination and thought maybe two were still "possible."

"I like Uncle Vito or even some of his ilk that Dominic might have really pissed off in some way," he said.

"Nope," she said. "Not him, even though I agree he was, or maybe still is, but no, I don't think so."

"So who?" he said.

"Margaret Patterson," she said triumphantly.

"The judge's secretary? No way," he said incredulously.

"Way, as the kids say," she replied.

"What do you know, or rather, what did you find out, about her," he asked.

"Margaret Patterson, if that is her real name," she said smiling, "and you're not going to believe this, is former CIA."

"What?" he exclaimed, a little too loudly for the small bar.

"Yes, sweet little Margaret," she said. "That's why I said if "Margaret Patterson" is her real name, and it probably isn't."

"This is getting good!" he exclaimed. "What did she do at the CIA?"

"Hold onto to your drink," she said. "That's classified."

"Holy shit!" he exclaimed, again too loudly. Nick, the bartender looked over at them and scowled, but then smiled because they had become regulars and after all, it was a bar.

"She really liked Judge Chalmers and worked for him for years," said Martin, "and she knew of Falucci because of his buying the survivorship interest and taking the Conners' house. She really does have a revenge motive."

"And, with her CIA contacts, even if not recent, she may have been able to contact someone she knew to do the "wet work," as I've heard they call it in the CIA."

"You mean "assassinations? he asked.

"Yes," she said, "and if this is what happened, and it might have, you can forget about going any further with this investigation. We have absolutely run into a stone wall."

"Yeah, I guess you're right about that," he said.

Chapter 72

"Agent Simon?" asked the voice on the telephone. "This is Bob Brady down at the lab. I have analyzed the non-tissue item you brought in and can verify that it is foreign matter. I have identified it as a 4 ML piece of a plastic bag of some kind. This is pretty heavy-duty and can be likened to the type of bags that contractors use when cleaning up debris from a demolition job. It is very strong and can hold brickbats, heavy metals and anything else without ripping. It won't withstand a bullet, however."

"So, in your opinion, is that how it was introduced into the bullet wound?" she asked.

"Yes, a bullet of a large caliber could have carried a piece of bag with it if the bag were over the gun when it was fired. We have been able to duplicate this in the lab if the bag was sufficiently thick enough," he said.

"Is this type of bag readily available?" she asked.

"Oh, yes, you can buy a roll of them at a Home Depot or a Lowe's," he said.

"And would the sound of a gun, specifically a .38, if it were in the bag when fired, be muffled somewhat?" she asked.

"Yes. While we didn't do any tests in that regard, the sound would be reduced somewhat," he said. "Do we need to do any comparison tests?"

"No, Bob, just the knowledge that the report from the pistol would be muffled somewhat is enough. That would explain why the neighbors didn't hear a gun shot," she said. "Thanks for this information. I don't suppose there is anyway of tracking who might have purchased this heavy-duty bag?"

"No, these bags are sold daily to anyone who wants them," he said, "and there is no way of identifying a specific purchase from a home store. As I said, this type of bag is bought and used by contractors. If you found the box, we could probably confirm that this piece came from a roll, and there might be 39 bags left on the roll. I think the box contains 40 bags. The person who used the bag to muffle the sound probably didn't have use for more than one."

"And, obviously, the bag would collect GSR from the shot, right?" she asked.

"Oh, for sure, or the shooter could have worn a rubber glove, but GSR would be inside the bag," Brady said.

"And could be rubbed onto a man's hand if the bag were turned inside out?" she asked.

"Oh, yes," he said, "without a doubt."

Having received this report from Brady at the FBI lab, she called Harvey and told him that his hunch was correct. The facts clearly evidenced that Judge Chalmers was murdered.

"So where does the FBI go with the case now?" he asked.

"That's up to the SAC," she said, "but I will brief him on the lab results as soon as we hang up. I'm pretty sure that he is going to open a case file to investigate the murder. This means the lab will be back at the condo very shortly looking for anything that may lead to the identity of the killer."

"And, does that turn your attention to Rocco?" asked Martin.

"He will be a suspect for sure, but thus far there is nothing to implicate him," she said.

"Yeah, I agree, but he is first on my list, having worked for Falucci in killing the Conners woman," said Martin.

"Yet, you have no proof of that either," she said. "But we can alert the SAC in Trenton. If Rocco does something that we can pick him up for, we can interrogate him about the death of Mrs. Conners. That would be a real shock to him since he probably thinks we don't know anything about it. Perhaps he might implicate Constantine. That might lead us to Falucci and the contract killing."

"Until then it's another cold case," Martin said, "but I'm not going to let it go. And we did prove that the judge was murdered. I can at least tell his daughter that, though I can't tell her what we found out about Margaret Patterson. That is really a winger with no proof whatsoever.

And, unfortunately, I will also have to give her the standard line about a resolution of her father's murder."

"What's that? she said.

"It's still under investigation," Martin said. "Let's stay in touch," he said.

"I would like that," said Rachel.

Epilogue

This novel is a work of fiction and has no relation to any person alive or dead, nor should any attempt be made to relate or connect any individual to the story.

The right of survivorship that exists within the property right of a tenancy by the entirety is Tennessee law, and may exist in the property laws of other states as well. This right is only divisible by a court having jurisdiction over the property and the husband and wife who own it by reason of their marriage.

If the marriage is dissolved and the property divided by a court resolving property issues between the divorcing parties, then the right ceases to exist.

As explained in this book, in a Chapter 7 bankruptcy case, the property may or may not be considered an asset to be dealt with by the Trustee assigned to the case. If only one of the married persons' files, then only that person's interest in property owned in the form of tenants by the entirety comes into the "bankruptcy estate." This creates the "right of survivorship" which is the subject plot of this novel, and it remains a salable interest should the Trustee decide to offer it for sale.

Ingram Content Group UK Ltd.
Milton Keynes UK
UKHW020738100323
418360UK00013B/1283